Remi and Alicia Can't Fall Again

Marty Vee

Newsletter Fun!

I love my newsletter, it's my favorite way to connect with my readers. Stay in the know about exciting news, upcoming releases, fun stuff, and freebies. https://www.subscribepage.com/martyvee

Marty Vee's Books

*G*rand Ridge

- **Grand Ridge is for Lovers**

- Hazel and Elijah Don't Get Caught (Prequel)

- Hazel and Elijah Find Out

- Remi and Alicia Can't Fall Again

A Grand Ridge Christmas
- Accidentally Under Your Tree

Grand Ridge Adjacent
Just...
- Just Fake Married

Other Books
- Truth or Daire

- All Roads to Carter

• You and Me in Quarantine

I hadn't seen a night sky like it in years—the Milky Way was a cloudy stripe through the ink.

Parking under the carport on my side of the duplex, I had carried my pillow and blanket inside. Furgie trailed behind me on the shoveled walk. The building's interior smelled like stale air and old carpet. Wood paneling lined the bottom half of every wall. In sock-covered feet, I climbed the stairs to the single bedroom and bathroom, then fell face first onto my temporary bed and quickly fell asleep with Furgie curled beside me.

She'd woken me just before seven itching so much the bed shook. When I couldn't fall back asleep, I took her outside before taking a shower with disappointing water pressure.

Probably should have confirmed where my clothes were beforehand, but I didn't.

I left a wet trail on the worn carpet as I rummaged through box after box. For some reason the stupid washcloth was still clenched in my fist. My body had progressed past goosebumps and a shiver every now and then to shivering constantly. There was a wood-burning stove in the corner opposite the sofa, but even if I did have the necessary fire-starting items, I never could get a good fire going. Instead, it mocked me and my frozen state.

"God, I'm like ten minutes away from being hypother—Ah ha!" I exclaimed, pulling a sweatshirt out from among framed photos and a silly old phone shaped like a rainbow and cloud. I slipped the sweatshirt over my head. The soft inside fabric brushed my torso but ended just above my navel.

"Well, it's something." I set my fists on my naked hips. "At least most of the boxes are open at this point."

On the sofa, Furgie snorted. Her snout wrinkled as she chewed on one of her hind legs. Crouching, I ran a hand down her back. "When I figure out how to leave this place with clothes on, we'll go. We might even be able to walk the wetlands over on Shelby Road and see what we're here to protect."

She continued gnawing.

Technically, my work didn't begin until Monday, but I could get a head start—like visiting local spaces for the vibe of the residence. Maybe I'd figure out the best way to gain footing in the town. It was a fine line to draw between convincing a community that I was here to help and not to be a busy body.

It'd be good to meet people before I started asking them to sign a petition for an emergency vote to rezone this parcel of land.

Furgie let out a few more snorts, her chewing intensified.

"Girl, you have been so itchy." I scratched my nails along her side, and she rolled onto her back. I gasped and pulled my hand back.

Her stomach was lobster colored and splotchy. It clashed with her coppery fur and was definitely a different color than usual.

"Oh my effing God! Furg, what the hell?"

She flicked her eyes to me, her eyebrows shifting, before curling to gnaw on herself again.

"No," I commanded, lifting her head. "You'll make yourself bleed."

The look on her face definitely claimed that would be better than what she was dealing with at the moment.

"I'll figure this out." I looked for my phone and to my immense surprise and relief, I spotted it on the side table.

Googling one handed, I continued searching for pants. My cell service was terrible and the blue line across the top wasn't moving at all. There didn't seem to be any way to increase my reception. It was so easy to take for granted the built-in amenities of urban life that rural settings just didn't have.

Pausing my investigation for clothes, I shuffled to a window, hoping that would help.

Apparently, my Wi-Fi needed to be hooked up yesterday.

I left my phone on the sill and went back to my quest for pants. Furgie continued itching, aggressively.

I found sweatpants packed with my cloth shopping bags. I still hadn't found a bra or underwear, and I did not have "bra-less" boobs. But at least returning to my phone next to the condensation dripping window wouldn't be torture anymore.

The Internet still wasn't working. I sent out a text to Sadie, my assistant and best friend: *Furgie is all red and itching like a mother-fucker. Can you text me the phone number for a vet clinic in the area?* I didn't have much hope the text would send but I was desperate.

"Okay, let's see if anyone nearby has unsecured Wi-Fi," I said to Furg.

She remained focused on her task to break through her skin either by claw or teeth.

It didn't take long for a list of three networks to appear on my screen. One of them had a really strong signal and didn't require a password, *EvrybdyHurts*.

I scanned the room with wide eyes. "Furguson, who are our neighbors? 'Everybody hurts'? That is alarming. I hope it's a sex dungeon or they're a dom or something. That is the only scenario I'm comfortable with."

Worrying on my lower lip, I wished I could Google if there was information that the person with the network could learn about me just by connecting to it. On the sofa, Furgie rolled to her other side to scratch with her opposite hind leg.

I sighed. "I'll sleep with a knife under my pillow."

Less than a minute later, I pressed the speaker of my phone to my ear.

"Grand Ridge Animal Clinic, this is Nora. How can I help you?" a polite but uninterested sounding receptionist answered.

"Hi, I'm hoping to get an appointment for my dog. I think she might be having an allergic reaction. She's itching like crazy, and she's all red."

"What's your availability?"

"Any time today."

"Oh, today?" I didn't like Nora's skepticism.

"If at all possible. At this rate, she won't have any skin left by tomorrow."

"Oh, no. Can I put you on hold for a moment? I'll see what I can do."

"I can hold."

Her voice changed, growing further away before cutting to silence, "Hey, Peace and Love, you wanna do a lady a solid?"

I puffed a laugh.

"You still there?" she asked a short time later.

"I am."

"One of our vets is willing to stay late for your appointment. If the situation becomes more urgent, come as soon as possible."

"Oh my gosh, thank you."

"No problem, so it's still a couple of hours from now, but I have you scheduled for four-thirty." She took my information and Furg's. The sofa that came with the rental creaked when I lowered onto the cushion next to her, gently restraining her from itching.

Hanging up, I brushed a hand down Furgie's side. Her leg kicked like it did when something tickled.

"Well, this is one way to introduce ourselves to the town."

Chapter Two

Remi

"Hey, Peace and Love, you wanna do a lady a solid?" Nora's question pulled me out of my wandering thoughts and back into the front office.

I'd already had the strangest morning, and it was still early. First, I'd woken up late last night to my new neighbor arriving. Then when she was outside with her dog, I'd caught a glimpse of the back of her head, and my blood ran cold. For just a second, in the dim morning light, I would have sworn that she was my ex-wife. But it was not the first time the sight of a stranger had stopped my heart, and the hairs on my arms stood on end. I exhaled my flurry of emotions through pursed lips.

Even after years of therapy, I still saw Alicia everywhere.

It couldn't be healthy. Not for my emotional or cardiovascular state. But there she was, right outside my front window. Except it wasn't her.

It never was.

I didn't stick around to identify what about the back of this woman's head reminded me so much of Alicia.

This woman—my new neighbor—had . . . too much red in her hair? It didn't matter. It wasn't her. Last I'd heard, she'd moved to Chicago. Why would she be in Grand Ridge, Michigan?

Anyway, I was still reeling from that ghost-like encounter. And then there was my work attire. Which was radioactive bright and could probably be seen from the moon. But that was what I got for thinking I could beat Nora in a bet. For my hubris, she got to pick my scrubs for a week. Today, I was in ankle-to-neck orange, yellow, and pink swirl-patterned tie-dye.

I ignored Hazel, my boss, laughing at me and the dry comments from Brooks, our large animal vet.

Instead, I asked, "There's a lady needing a solid?"

"Yeah, she thinks her dog is having an allergic reaction."

Hazel sat up straighter, the smile slipped from her face. "Is it having a hard time breathing?"

"She didn't say so, just a lot of itching," Nora said.

I snatched my tablet off its charger and powered it up. "What do I have available?"

"Everyone is fully booked. But you're scheduled early to leave, it'd have to be after your last appointment."

"I can do that."

"Make sure she knows to come in as soon as possible if the reaction becomes an emergency."

Nora went back to her phone call.

Brooks tilted his head and narrowed his eyes at me.

"What?" I knew he was going to make some shitty comment about my scrubs. It's not like I could forget what I was wearing with the colors reflecting on my tablet screen and making it hard to read.

"I just realized what you remind me of."

Nora hung up the phone and typed in a quick, confident rhythm on her keyboard.

Knowing I was about to be roasted, I asked anyway, "What is that?"

"I had a poster like you on my wall in elementary school."

"Oh shit, you did!" Nora's fingers stopped their pounding and her eyes went wide. "If you looked at it just right, you could see a horse running on a beach."

"Relaxing." He jerked his chin up.

Hazel shook her head. "It's just so much tie-dye."

"Where's the headband?" Nora swiveled her chair.

I shoved my hand in my pocket but didn't pull out the fake leather strap right away. "Do I really have to wear it?"

"You made the bet."

"It doesn't look right with how short my hair is."

"I think being concerned about your appearance at this point is a bit silly," Hazel remarked.

Nora squinted. "Let me see it. I'll decide."

"And your hair isn't that short," Hazel continued. "It's around your cheekbones."

I shoved the stretchy, weirdly patterned headband over my hair and across my forehead.

For a moment, they only stared, before Brooks commented, "That is a look."

"I don't think your hair being short is the problem," Nora deadpanned.

Pursing her lips, Hazel considered me. "I never realized how big your head is."

"I'm a big guy." It was an unnecessary thing to say. They could all see that for themselves.

"You can take the headband off," Nora offered. "It's stretched within an inch of its life, anyway."

Brooks checked his watch. "Well, this was worth me being three minutes late to the Higgins farm. I gotta go."

"I'm glad you could be here for this," I said to my tablet screen.

"You're gonna want to see tomorrow too. It's my favorite," Nora called to his retreating back, his boots squeaking on the tile floor.

A mixture of apprehension and curiosity made my palms sweat, as my mind's eye conjured the image of the last paper bag sitting on my dresser. I could have peeked but not knowing what flavor of outlandish scrubs waited for me each day had been kinda fun. A little surprise. Even if I looked extra ridiculous today, at least it created a difference from day to day.

When I'd opened yesterday's bag, I'd thought she'd misunderstood the assignment. The sky-blue scrubs had seemed completely normal until I turned over the shirt and found "Swiftie" scrawled there. Which would have been fine, but the lyrics, "I did something bad," were written across my ass. And that really distinguished the whole look. I tried wearing a sweater tied around my waist but it inevitably fell off due to how much bending over veterinarian work calls for.

Knowing Nora, whatever was in the last bag would be worse even than today's.

Unimaginable.

"Unlock the door, will you?" Hazel called.

Brooks threw a wave over his shoulder and pushed through the vestibule door.

Turning my focus to my tablet, I scrolled through my appointments.

"Shit," I hissed reading the last name of the day.

"I know, it sucks." Nora's shoulders slumped.

A crease formed between Hazel's eyebrows. "What's wrong?"

"Lily Nelson is bringing Rocko in," I explained.

"I thought you'd already fulfilled your auction commitment," Hazel said.

"He did." Nora spoke to her computer monitor without pausing in her work. "I clarified that she'd be paying for this one."

Nora's undertones of irritation were obvious in the appointment notes. *Owner stated a need for appointment due to obedience issues. It was made clear to owner that we do not offer obedience training. Owner remained insistent to keep appointment as scheduled. Owner was re-emailed a list of American Kennel Club certified obedience trainers in the area.*

In October, the clinic had thrown a bachelor auction to raise money for the local humane society. Instead of selling dates, the men of the town sold our trades. *I* had offered three free vet visits. As soon as betting began, Lily started bidding aggressively. In the moment, I was having a good time, and I didn't think anything of it. Until, for weeks afterward, Lily and I were a source of gossip. The folks of Grand Ridge loved to murmur about their neighbors. I would think they were out of line if Lily had *had* a pet when she'd bought my vet package.

By the time of her first appointment, she'd adopted a year and a half old Mastiff-Lab mix with behavioral issues: Rocko.

Anytime I was near them, I wasn't sure who I pitied more, her or Rocko.

He was hyper and gigantic. Poor Lily had been dragged through multiple snowbanks.

I felt bad for her, really. But her advances toward me were growing as aggressive as her auction bidding had been and turning her down was getting embarrassing. Lily was great in a lot of ways. She had a good job. She was beautiful—big gray eyes; full, pouty mouth; tall; curvy. We were both single and similar ages. When I had first moved to Grand Ridge, I'd considered starting a casual friends-with-benefits thing with her. But the town didn't really do casual: a first date was a near-marriage proposal.

Since moving here, my dating life had gone pretty dry. A far cry from my time in Phoenix.

"We're just going over obedience again?" I asked, not expecting anyone to have an answer.

Hazel sucked her lips between her teeth.

Glancing over her shoulder, Nora said, "You know, the scrubs might put an end to whatever it is she has planned."

"You think so?" I grabbed the hem of my shirt and pulled it away from my body to get a better, and unnecessary, look. "They're just scrubs."

"If anything could, it's them."

Chapter Three
Alicia

There was not a whole lot to do in early February in a town this size, especially having a thirty-pound cocker spaniel in tow. My options were limited. But I was starving and there wasn't any food at my place. I couldn't leave Furgie alone; her symptoms hadn't gotten worse, but they hadn't gotten better.

Sadie and I had Googled giving Furgie an over-the-counter medication. It turned out that I could, but also couldn't, and also probably don't.

Then we talked about how much we missed each other already, until the crushed granola bar I'd found at the bottom of my purse stopped keeping my ravenous hunger at bay. There were two possible places that I might be able to get food and bring Furgie, a rustically trendy bar and an eclectically trendy coffee shop.

If both failed me, I would have to do a drive-through. But I really wanted to meet a Grand Ridge person.

Parking my SUV outside of Country Grounds Café, I took hold of the leash. The cold snapped at my cheekbones as we rushed to the front door. The warm air just inside smelled of espresso and baked goods—I sent up a silent prayer that they wouldn't tell me to get my dog out of there and kick dirt. Or snow, I guess.

"Hi," a woman even taller than me called from behind the counter.

Gesturing to the leash around my wrist, I asked, "Is it okay for me to have her here?"

"Of course." The smile on her face was as wide and welcoming as the decor of her place. There were used mugs stacked in a bin on top of the trash can, but I was the only customer at the moment. There were shelves on the wall with knickknacks for sale. And two loveseats facing a shared coffee table. On the far back wall was a huge poster of a floral meadow with a poorly photo-shopped crystal blue unicorn rearing. The café's name was at the top, and under the hooves it read, *Our grounds are magic.*

I was charmed.

She hooked her arm, welcoming me in. "What can I help you with?"

"I just moved in, and I don't have any food at my place. Are you serving your sandwiches?"

"It's not the full menu that we have during summer, but I have a couple I can do. I have soup too."

My shoulders sagged. "You're a saint."

"The Patron Saint of Soups on a Cold Day." She grinned.

I snorted. Furgie sniffed the air as we walked to the counter.

It didn't take long to place my order. A few minutes later, she handed me my coffee. I held it between my chilled fingers and breathed in the comforting smell.

She raised her voice to be heard with her back to me as she prepared my food. "So, what brings you to Grand Ridge?"

Moment of truth. At my past jobs, residents either loved hearing that I was there for nature conservation or resented me for it.

"There's a wetland over on the northwest side, just outside of city limits, and I'm here to stop it from being developed."

She paused and tilted her head. "Over by the Creger's?"

"I'm not sure who lives over there, it's an equestrian therapy place."

Nodding, she went back to her work. "Yeah, I know exactly where it's at."

I couldn't read her reaction, and I didn't want the conversation to go south, so I changed the subject. "Is this your café?"

"It is. I opened it almost six years ago."

"I'm in love with it."

"Me too." She beamed over her shoulder. "Your dog is so cute. What's her name?"

"Furgie."

"Like the toy from the early 2000s?"

"Those were Furby's."

"God, those were terrifying."

"Horrifying." I looked down at my dog, scratching. Again.

"Are you renting?"

I gestured vaguely in the direction of my place. "Yeah, it's over that way."

The expression grew distant. "Ol' Terrance Miller's place?"

Shrugging, I said, "My employer handled my lease."

"It's a duplex? Your neighbor is like . . . *really* handsome."

"I have a sneaking suspicion that he's a total smoke show, but I've only seen his shoulders from behind. And they were"—I held my arms ridiculously wide—"broad."

"That's doc-too-hottie."

"Oh, he's a doctor?" I lifted an eyebrow.

"Veterinarian."

"Really?" My stomach flipped. I tried to recall the shape of his shoulders in my mind's eye. The stretch of brown corduroy. The span of his shoulders had been . . . *too* wide. There had to be plenty of rather large, hot veterinarians. Not just the one. It was just a thing that my brain did every once in a while—conjure up an unrealistic scenario that might put me face-to-face with my ex-husband. But the odds of him moving back to Michigan and living in the other half of my duplex were practically impossible. Scratch that, completely impossible.

Pulling myself out of a horrifying mental exercise was made easier by the ringing of the bell over the door. Furgie paused in her itching to look in the direction of the newcomer. It was instinct that drew my eyes to follow the sound, but it was the flirtatious smile on the beautiful man's face that made me look away. This guy was a knockout—blue eyes so bright they were practically a light source, black hair, and dark scruff on his jaw.

Behind the counter, the woman tossed her long brown braid behind her shoulder. "Hey, Strauss."

"Millie, how's the family?" He leaned a hip against the counter, keeping his body language open to bring me into the conversation.

"They're good." Millie carried a tray with my club sandwich and a steaming bowl of corn chowder to my table.

"Glad to hear it."

There were a few moments where the only sound was plates clattering together, before Millie said, "Did you see the animal clinic's page this morning."

Laughing, he shook his head. "What bet did that man lose?"

"I don't know but I'd make a bet with the devil before Nora."

"Giant fool." The man jerked his head toward my food Millie was carrying to me. "That looks good."

Fixing my most polite and not at all encouraging grin on my face, I agreed. "It does."

"Mind making me the same thing, Mill?"

"Sure thing, Sterl."

His grin grew even wider, as if encouraged by the sarcasm in her voice. "You're a gem, Mih."

She snorted. "You're a snot, Ster."

He fixed those incredibly blue eyes at me, and I wondered if he had ever modeled. Even in a Carhartt jacket and worn jeans, he was artfully beautiful. Not my normal type, but he was easy to appreciate. I had my rules, anyway. Really just the one: No fraternizing with the men folk.

Extending a hand, he introduced himself. "I'm Sterling."

"Pleasure. I'm Alicia."

"Nice to meet you."

"She was just telling me that there's some sort of development going in over by Creger stables," Millie explained. I still didn't have a read on how she felt about it, but the news was going to get around now. It was hard to be a stranger in these communities. It could be lonely. And when they didn't want me around, the isolation could feel a bit suffocating.

The tags on Furgie's collar jangled.

I wouldn't be completely alone.

A crease formed between his eyebrows. "Whereabouts?"

"You know that marsh that Mr. Lewell did the mud crawl in a few years back?" Millie sliced a tomato and spoke as if she didn't have any feeling about the land at all. Maybe she didn't.

"For the theater department?"

"Mm." She nodded.

They were having a conversation that I couldn't decipher. Insider telepathy that I wasn't privy to as an outsider.

When Sterling fixed his eyes on me again, they carried a sharp focus they hadn't before. "What are you planning on developing there?"

"I work for a non-profit, the Great Lakes Water Protection Agency. So, I'm here to protect the marshland."

His gaze softened. The easy smile returned to his face. "Nice."

The knot that had formed in my gut loosened. Clearly, he felt positive about the job I was here to do.

"So, you're like"—his grin went lopsided. Behind him, Millie rolled her eyes—"a total badass."

"Yes," I laughed. "I am a total badass."

It didn't mean that I'd be able to save the marsh, though. The cards were stacked against me on this one.

Chapter Four

Remi

"Have you implemented the exercise routine we discussed at our last appointment?" I asked to the top of Lily's head. Bending, I ran a hand down Rocko's brindle coat. He leaned against my thigh, his pink tongue hanging out of his mouth.

"I just don't have time in my schedule." Lily spoke down to her phone, her fingers pounding on the screen.

"But you'd like an improvement in his behavior?" Keeping my voice clear of judgment was challenging.

She glanced up and then away again. "Yes."

Much like the bets I would no longer accept from Nora, I would never question her intuition. Lily refused to look directly at me. In our past appointments, she'd rubbed her side-boob on my arm so much it couldn't be a mistake. I'd smell like her floral perfume for the rest of the day. Not today, though.

When she'd laid her eyes on me, a seductive smile had slipped from her face, and her upper lip had curled in disgust.

I'd never appreciated feeling unattractive before.

"I would suggest those exercises; I think he'd really respond to them. I know it's a time commitment, but he's eager to please. He just has so much energy."

Her eyes grew, almost comically, with desperate hope. "Will that fix him?"

"There doesn't seem to be anything wrong with him. He just needs training."

"I'm just really busy right now. What about a medication? Is there a medication I could give him instead?"

I refrained from pointing out that she'd found time to visit me once a week for the past four. "I would only suggest medicine for a medical intervention. I know we've talked about this before, but being such a large dog, there's less room for error. Rocko doing normal dog things, jumping on a kid, for example, could put him and *you* in trouble. He's a normal, excitable, adolescent dog. I think he'd respond well to obedience classes."

She pouted, tilting her head to one side. "I just wish I had someone to help me, you know?"

Uh-oh. The magic of the scrubs was wearing off.

I avoided her subtext. "Is there a reason you got such a big dog?"

"I like big . . . *dogs.*"

I pinched my lips between my teeth, my eyebrows drawn together. Was she comparing me to a dog? Was I supposed to project myself onto Rocko? Or was she making a sexual innuendo, and "dogs" was being used to replace "penis?"

At a loss, all I could say was, "Well, you have a big dog now. I don't see how another appointment here could help you. My suggestion is obedience training."

She looked at me through her eyelashes, her bottom lip plumped out. "Do you think you could help me with that? I could cook you dinner. What's your favorite dish?"

Fuck.

My fingers paused scratching behind Rocko's ear, and he barked in protest. It bounced off the walls, rattling my eardrums.

"I would not suggest myself for that. You really should refer to the list Nora emailed," I responded.

"Then why don't I cook you dinner, anyway? A thank you for the free visits."

"Uh, I appreciate that. But it's not necessary."

She lifted a delicate shoulder. "Let's not call it a thank you, then. We'll call it a date."

"I don't think that's a good idea. I'm Rocko's vet. We shouldn't muddy the waters."

God, I was pulling at straws. If I limited my dating options based on whose pet I took care of, I'd be lucky if there were three single women left in the county. But my immediate needs outweighed logic.

"The water's already muddy, Remi," she purred.

I straightened, ignoring Rocko's protest, and crossed my arms over my chest. I resisted rolling my eyes, but just barely. Pulling on every ounce of patience I had, I searched for the kindest way to let Lily down.

A few minutes later, Lily pulled her dog toward the employee entrance yelling, "Someday you're going to realize what a mistake you've made!"

Rocko's claws scraped on the tile. He jumped and barked around her with his tail wagging. Fighting against him, she struggled for every foot she gained toward the back door.

"I'm sure I will." I grimaced at the floor under my no-slip shoes. Letting her down hadn't gone well, no matter how gentle I tried to be.

"And I won't be waiting around for you."

Leaping, Rocko bumped into her hip, pushing her into the wall. "Jesus Christ on a cross, Rocko!"

I took a half step toward her. "Are you okay?"

The glare she sliced my way stopped me in my tracks. "This is going to be the biggest mistake of your life."

Lily pulled an excited Rocko through the back door, her phone pressed to her ear.

I scraped a palm down my face, offering up a thank you to the universe that my appointments were done for the day. With my head hanging, and my heart thudding dully in my chest, I turned for the front office and fell back against the doorjamb—my weight a bit too heavy to bear at the moment.

There was a fist clenched around my chest. Something in the past few minutes, or maybe it was residual from my glimpse of my new neighbor from the morning, but a memory I hated revisiting fought for the surface of my mind. Rain dripping from the russet strands of Alicia's hair.

A door closing, severing the worn threads that tied us together.

I was still standing on the other side of it.

Nora half-stood, half-leaned on the desk behind her, an apologetic twist to her mouth when I walked into the front office. "That was rough."

"I think she's done making unnecessary appointments . . . or using us for veterinary care."

"Meh." Shrugging, Nora said, "She'll chill out in a day or two. Your last appointment is in exam room one."

I looked up with wide eyes. "No. I thought that was my last appointment."

"Remember the emergency? The allergic cocker spaniel."

"Shit." My arms hung limp at my side. I rescinded my thank you to the universe. "Right. Cool."

"I sent her chart to your tablet."

"Thanks." With my thumb and index, I rubbed circles at the tension above my eyebrows. "I guess it's a vet visit and a show."

She patted my arm. "Sometimes our embarrassment is public."

I snorted. "That's comforting."

"Oh, your friend Owen commented '*groovy*' to your picture I posted earlier."

A smile broke across my face. "You're really driving home your 'sometimes embarrassment is public' point, aren't you?"

"Seems to be the theme."

"Reply a middle finger emoji, will you?"

"Sure thing."

I tucked my tablet under my arm and took a step backward into the hallway. Just outside of the door, I paused. Trying to put the past few minutes behind me, I psyched myself up for a new patient. But more than the humiliation, the unwanted resurfacing of my biggest failure lingered.

Regret was a weight on my chest, my lungs too tight to fill fully. It was coming home to an empty house, and a string of meaningless sex. Regret was missing one person too much to consider finding someone new. Being single could be lonely. It was okay, though. For now. But how much longer would now be?

Falling required a leap, and I hadn't been brave enough to stray from the safety of my path for years. In so many ways, I'd never been more emotionally available in my life, but only with my existing relationships. Ones where the dynamic was set. Where I felt secure.

Someone unproven?

With the battered remains of my heart?

I didn't think so.

Decked shoulder to ankle in tie-dye, having just turned down Lily's advances and been chewed out for it, while having an existential crisis, I opened the door to exam room one. The tablet screen displayed the dog's weight, and name, but little else.

There was a gasp from within the room before a plastic jar of dog treats scattered on the tile floor. The little dog startled at the owner's feet and sniffed one of the Milk-Bones. I took a deep breath and blew it out between pursed lips. It wasn't a big deal, but after the onslaught of the last few minutes my threshold for irritation was pretty low.

"Ugh . . ." the woman groaned. A curtain of russet waves concealed her face, except for the point of her chin. Her fingertips pressed to her lips. There was something familiar about her hair. The color. The texture.

The memory loomed. As if there was something important I was forgetting.

My growing dread was calmed as realization dawned. My neighbor from this morning. The one that had stopped my heart looking so much like Alicia.

But it was never Alicia.

Sighing, I lowered to one knee. "It's okay."

I scooped up the treats, and they fell back into the jar with little thuds. The dog smelled the air, testing out my scent. I extended my arm to her with a little bone in my palm. "Hey there, girl. Want one?"

She sat back and began itching, looking up at her owner, who hadn't moved an inch.

"Not for you? That's okay, I've got better stuff." I assured the dog.

Still on one knee, I offered my hand to the woman. "Would you take—"

My throat choked close. Gold spots speckled my vision. Tingles shot through my fingers and arms.

How?

And I was offering her a fucking dog treat.

I croaked a single broken word. "Leese?"

Chapter Five

Alicia

"Leese?" There were new wrinkles at the corner of Remi's eyes. But it was unmistakably him. His broad shoulders, his tall frame. The curl of his upper lip, and the peaks of his cupid's bow. High cheekbones, and the sharp, straight hook of his nose.

This man.

Here?

The man.

Here?

His eyes the color of the midnight sky, darted around the room. A room filled with the clean, sweet smell of tobacco from the soap he apparently still used. A dog treat rested on the familiar lines of his calloused palm.

"Yeah, I work here," he explained. He dropped the Milk-Bone to the floor and pushed himself to stand. With unsteady legs he took a few steps backward.

At least he wasn't on one knee anymore. Memory overlapping the present had been . . . *a lot* . . . on top of a shit ton.

So, not great.

"Since when?" I ignored the fact that I didn't know how long I'd been speaking out loud or what I might have said.

"A couple of years."

"But Arizona . . ."

His eyes flicked to mine and then to the floor. He hadn't told me he'd moved, just like he hadn't told me he'd moved back. We'd parted ways like two people playing chicken: the first to make contact lost. I'd distanced myself from the friends we had in common. In twelve interminable months, I didn't have any remaining connections to him. No more strings tying us together.

It'd been self-preservation, as much as spite.

A defense against the bombardment of grief and loss that flooded my system whenever his name was mentioned. But now I was desensitized to his existence.

And his existence was *here*.

"I moved a couple of years ago." He rubbed a palm along his jaw, a nervous habit. "My friend, uh, Hazel, do you remember Hazel?"

I nodded, even though I was still searching the recesses of my mind. A nice woman, who mostly kept to herself. Smart. Competent. Remi always had a soft spot for quiet people—possibly why we never worked out. He needed me to be quieter. I needed . . . *more*. More reassurance. More connection. More of him.

My mouth still hung open. I cupped my throat, my bent elbow supported by my other hand.

"Uh, she owns this place."

I pointed at the floor beneath our feet.

"Yeah." His head jerked to look at something over his shoulder.

"Wow. She's young." She was a couple of years younger than us. She couldn't be thirty yet.

His eyes never really fell on me. As soon as they wandered in my direction, they'd snap somewhere else. Anywhere else.

"Yeah. Anyway, she asked me to work here, and Mom wanted me to move back, and Mitch had a kid—"

"You're an uncle?" I interrupted. I couldn't tell if this word vomit was soothing or overwhelming. At least, he seemed as unsettled by me as I was by him.

"Yeah. Maisey."

"I love that name."

"I know."

Of course, he knew. We'd discussed baby names from time-to-time. My mind conjuring the image of him scooping up our blue-eyed, red-haired future child in his impossibly gentle hands was always right there as we talked. Maybe after we moved to East Lansing for his schooling. Maybe after I started working in environmental conservation. Maybe after he graduated.

Maybe after we learned to actually communicate.

But no.

He had a little Maisey to dote over, and that was at once beautiful and eviscerating.

I was cored out. Husked.

His Adam's apple bobbed. "Uh, yeah, she'll be two in spring. She's really cute."

"I bet." I sounded empty.

"Uh-huh." Finally, his eyes swept up and down my body as if he was landing back inside of his mind from wherever he'd gone. "What are you doing here?"

"My dog."

"Right." He blinked a few times, and I realized he meant in Michigan, but he recovered before I could explain. "Your dog."

"Furgie."

He puffed a laugh. "Furry Furg?"

One corner of my mouth twitched. "Sometimes. Usually Furguson. She's a stately girl."

"Clearly discerning in her treat of choice."

Amusement flickered—a tiny flame snuffed out by dark billowy smoke from a larger fire. Years ago, it'd blazed through me, leaving behind soot covered sticks and ashes.

Emotions were shifting too quickly inside of my chest. They must have flashed across my face, because Remi fell back on his heel as if pushed. Was it my rage at being surprised by him? The echo of the all-consuming pain dredged to the surface after five years? Or was it the moment something easy passed between us? Something that felt more dangerous than all the rest of it.

He stared at my shoes with his mouth open, breathing heavily.

Somewhere in the room, a clock ticked away.

Finally, he said, "So, what's going on with Furguson?"

My thoughts lagged for a few more moments, before I explained. Remi lowered to the tile floor, sitting with his back to the wall. He extended his hand to Furg, welcoming her to smell him. The movement was so natural. A behavior ingrained in his process, taking his hulking form and becoming a less intimidating version of himself for my dog.

Being exactly the veterinarian he'd always aspired to be.

In a strange out of body like experience, I listed her symptoms. My mouth spoke while my mind worked in multiple streams. There was the repeated mantra of, "*What the fuck is happening?*" that I was trying to ignore. And the recollection of my naivete. I'd been just a few minutes ago snickering at the drama I could overhear in the hallway. Former lovers gone sour.

I'd texted Sadie, giggling silently to myself.

Sadie: Is he hot?

Me: I haven't seen him yet. But this lady is pissed. She is literally screaming.

Sadie: I kind of admire her for it. I could never.

Me: Me either.

Then the door opened and startlingly bright scrubs entered the room. And then his face.

Remi was tender and calming with Furgie. At the end of the appointment, his eyes flicked up to me then away, again. Where he couldn't seem to lay his eyes on me, I couldn't take mine away from him. The dusting of reddish blond hair on the back of his hands was a bit thicker. His jaw was a little wider too. He had the audacity to have a face that had gone from hot to hotter. His boyish softness replaced with the masculine strength of a grown ass man. The audacity might have continued on to his body, but that was hard to tell with the distracting swirling nature of his clothes.

God, if I'm noticing him, is he noticing me?

It was such a mind fuck.

I was thicker and softer than I had been. Wrinkles were forming around my eyes and mouth. I was trying to unpack all the societal pressure to never age and not let it be a part of my self-worth. But it was still there.

Did he see all the ways I'd changed?

Don't care, I ordered myself. *Please, don't care.*

It must have only taken a couple of minutes, but it felt like an eternity for him to break the silence in the room. He gestured to the bright red of Furgie's stomach. "It's an allergy flair. Obviously, she's in a new environment. We can give her antibiotics that'll help with the itching and clear up the rash. And some conditioning spray."

I jerked forward, just then realizing I'd never taken a seat. I'd stood awkwardly the whole appointment, looming over him like an agitated vulture. "Will it come back?"

He held out a hand, and for a terrifying moment, I thought he might run it down my arm. When it just remained palm out, I might have missed the touch I didn't get. Because everything inside of me was in turmoil, and there was no way to satisfy any part of me.

"It shouldn't, but if it does we'll get her on a daily medicine," he explained. "We'll be okay. I'll get you a prescription for antibiotics. Where would you like it sent?"

His use of the word, *we'll* was a bit triggering, but what wasn't in this nightmare situation? I shrugged. "I have no idea."

"I'll send it to the pharmacy here in town, if that's okay?"

"Yeah, absolutely. Thank you."

Not long after, I walked through the door he held open. I had to pass close enough to him to feel the heat coming off his body. My snow boots squeaked with each step. Furgie's leash swung into my leg. It taxed my depleted energy to make eye contact as I paid, but I forced myself to. The receptionist had large, round brown eyes. They flicked between me and Remi. It didn't take sharp intelligence to see that we were both . . . *off*. But her gaze assessed us.

"Thank you, again," I struggled to say.

He nodded, his jaw tight.

"Of course, let us know if you need anything else," she said.

I turned. The lobby floated past me.

When I was in the vestibule, she whispered behind my back, "What happened?"

He didn't answer.

What did *happen?*

"Are you okay?" The glass door to the lobby muffled her voice.

I couldn't see his reaction—if he shook his head, or shrugged, or nodded. I didn't think he responded verbally. But then there was a loud buzzing in my ears. I couldn't remember where I put my keys. I patted my coat pockets, dug through my purse, and then did the whole thing again.

Be here somewhere, I silently begged my keys. *I cannot go back in there*.

My stomach did a sickening back flip as she asked, "You out here just breakin' hearts?"

But there'd been two sets of hands ripping and pulling our hearts to shreds. Two people too self-righteous to stop our bullshit. Too many cuts to keep us from hemorrhaging.

I was on the other side of it. The side where it didn't hurt so much anymore. Or I had been before he walked into that examination room. Now I was all turned around.

My heart broken and the memory of falling in love with him given a fresh coat of paint. Graphic. Present.

Falling in love with Remi had been the easy part. It was everything that followed that went totally tits up.

Finally, I found my keys tucked in my coat pocket. They jangled, their teeth biting my fingers, and pushed the exterior door open. The blast of frozen dry air was a welcome relief against my hot face.

His chuckle was bitter and completely void of humor. "Not right now, okay, Nora?"

He sounded as rung out as I felt.

Chapter Six

Alicia

"This is fine," I whispered to my windshield, as the sun set in gorgeous shades of bright gold and deep purple. The branches of the trees hung heavy with snow reflecting the sky.

My ex-husband worked in this little town.

He'd been on one knee.

He had a Maisey.

He was good at his job.

He was still hot. Bullshit.

"Where was death when you needed it?"

God, I'm in pieces.

Resisting the urge to cyberstalk him over the past five years had been . . . challenging—and let's be real, in the first two years, unsuccessful. But after seeing him tagged in a few too many photos with beautiful women hanging on his arms, I'd found a therapist to help me resist that particular impulse.

It was the right choice. I was struggling to move on, and every time I walked down that particular Internet path, I'd end up wallowing, pouring salt into old wounds, and never letting them heal.

But if I hadn't given up that little toxic behavior, I wouldn't have been blindsided today. I would have known.

Furgie fidgeted in the front passenger seat. She'd been itching when I parked in front of the pharmacy to dash into the bone chilling cold just to find the doors to the establishment locked.

I was accustomed to city hours. But I guessed this was the hard way to remember places like this worked on a different schedule.

But then, a middle-aged woman with long dark hair streaked with silver pushed open the door I'd just turned away from. "You here from the vet clinic?"

I must have looked ridiculous blinking at her with my mouth open. "Uh, yeah."

"Come on in."

A few minutes later, I paid, and she handed me a paper bag.

"You're lucky, Remi called in the nick of time, I was just locking up."

A frantic trill of a laugh fell out of my mouth.

Lucky?

She stared at me a bit more apprehensive than she'd been just a moment before. It was as if she expected something from me, but I didn't know what I was supposed to do.

After a few moments she asked, "Is there anything else I can help you with?"

"Oh." I shook the bag in my hand rattling the pills inside. "No. Thank you."

Hurrying back outside, I took hold of my driver's side door. The hinges creaked and warm air hit my skin as I slid back into my seat. The drive back to my duplex was easy. They had scraped the main roads clear of snow, piling it into frozen waves along the shoulders.

I wanted to be home so badly. Not this new rental. But Chicago. I wanted to grab a basket of fries and a seltzer with Sadie and tell her this wild AF story where I was face-to-face with the man who had been the foundation of my life. How when that foundation had been blasted apart, it wasn't a rocky mess underneath but a black hole that sucked me through. It rearranged all my molecules, and when I shot out the other side, I was still me, but completely different.

I was a tightly wound bundle of frayed emotions and confusion.

I didn't want to be alone through this.

There was a painful drilling pressure in my sternum. He was the most familiar stranger, when there had been a time that I knew everything about him. There had been a time when he was my favorite person. There had been a time we'd entwined our futures.

Back before our relationship died a death of a thousand cuts, one petty infraction after another. So many stupid arguments about how I felt ignored and he felt like he couldn't do enough to make me happy. Mornings of his silent treatment, turned into nights of me out dancing with my friends ignoring his calls and texts. Repeated. Chiseling away at our affection and patience.

Our marriage wasn't well. Then it was a feeble thing, too weak to stand.

I was so angry and immature. Outraged.

Desperate for his attention. And spiteful.

When I filed for the divorce papers, I wanted him to call my bluff.

But he'd signed them and closed the door in my face.

Seeing him . . . Old wounds, new salt.

Patting Furgie's head, I looked for comfort just as much as I gave it. We'd curl up on the bed my employer had rented and rest.

Perhaps, I just needed perspective. Yes, it was a small town, but what was the likelihood of me running into him? It had to be pretty low. If we found ourselves at the same establishment, we'd just avoid each other.

This could be good. He couldn't surprise me again. Now that I knew he was here I'd always be on guard.

I turned onto my driveway and came to an abrupt halt. At the sight of long legs no longer clad in tie-dye, I almost put my car in reverse. Even from this distance, with his back to me, I'd recognize him anywhere.

"What fresh hell is this?" I demanded.

Standing outside of my front door with his shoulders shrugged toward his ears and his hands buried into the pockets of his jeans was Remi.

I was torn between apprehension, and the knowledge that he'd violated my privacy this way. How did he get my address? Was it from my paperwork? But why? There was no way he wanted to relive that awkward encounter. I sure as hell didn't.

He wasn't even wearing a coat, just a long-sleeve, navy T-shirt.

Parking under my carport, I drummed my fingers on the steering wheel before deciding that I'd just let him know to forget my address. Whatever reason brought him to my front door, he could take it back home with him.

I didn't need to know . . .

I kinda wanted to know . . .

It could at least wait until tomorrow when I wasn't in such a weird state of mind.

Furgie and I hurried through the side door into the kitchen with it's dark cabinets and a stack of broken-down cardboard boxes stacked next to the fridge. The slip of my laces untying seemed loud in the silence of my duplex as I waited for the sound of his fist thudding on the door.

Why isn't he knocking?

I kicked my boots off. My house slippers were colder than my feet, but I put them on anyway. I moved through the kitchen with its dark cabinets to the living room. Furgie had hopped onto the sofa and curled up.

And I waited.

Grabbing one of her dog treats, I smooshed it around an antibiotic.

And waited.

She took the treat and pill with the little nub of her tail wagging excitedly.

My teeth were clenched so tight I was probably causing damage to my molars.

Jesus Christ, knock on the door.

He knew I was here. He'd seen me pull up. So, why wasn't he knocking on the door? I wanted this over with.

This being a second encounter with the lost love of my life.

It was like he'd ripped my chest open and pointed at the place he still occupied. I was over him. But only in the most technical terms. I dated. I worked. I had friends and a life. I was fulfilled.

There was just . . . Loving him had changed me.

Losing him had changed me again.

I'd developed into who I was because of my relationship with him.

With all of that, I didn't know how to make his presence outside of my door not matter.

His lack of knocking felt passive aggressive, just like when he'd say he wasn't mad, then go days without talking to me until he would blow up about something stupid like makeup on the bathroom counter. I'd hated it then, just like I hated it now. But back then I would have been passively antagonistic back.

Not now, not today.

My slipper-covered march to the front door was loud enough that Remi looked up and met my narrowed eyes through the window. His brow knit together in a cringe, as if preparing for impact, and he sure as hell should because I was coming in hot.

I swung the door open fast enough to make a whooshing sound and blow the strands of his hair away from his face. I ignored the gush of freezing wind.

My irritated words came out in quick, angry puffs of steam. "Remi Akerman, I don't know what you thought pilfering my address off of medical forms—which hugely violates my privacy, and you know that! Regardless of how poor that decision was, I was going to *politely* tell you to go home. But you sitting out here *waiting* for me to address you, and not even giving me the courtesy of ringing the doorbell? I have decided to be *rude*. Whatever bad idea has brought you here, turn around and take it home."

He pulled his lips to one side squinting an eye shut and letting out a rumbling groan.

I held up a manicured finger. "No, don't stand there groaning like a bear. Go. Home."

"I can explain—" he started, but I cut him off.

"No. No excuses. I never would have thought that you'd behave so creepy—because you know this *is* creepy." I was speaking so quickly all my words strung together into one.

"It is, the way you're seeing it, it is creepy."

I nearly screamed, "*The way I'm seeing it?!*"

I paced a few steps toward him and then back, my arms crossed over my chest. "Reality, that's what I'm seeing. What is so important that you came to my house? My God, if you are going to abuse personal information, you could start with my phone number and text me. We could have met in a public place and talked about whatever is going on. *What* could be so important? Did you secretly have my baby? Are you here to tell me I have a four-year-old?"

He held out a calming hand. " 'Licia, I swear I can explain."

"Not today, you can't. Today I don't have ears for it. Go. Home." I gestured wildly to anywhere that wasn't here.

"Leese." The firm edge of his tone cut whatever I was about to say off from the tip of my tongue. His shoulders sagged, and the ends of his eyebrows turned down. With a shake of his head, he said, "I am home. But I'm locked out."

My breath caught. Even with my mind rejecting to comprehend his words, I remembered broad shoulders from this morning and the little remark Millie from the café had made. I looked over my shoulder to see the door positioned maybe two feet away from mine. There was a snow-covered Adirondack chair next to it.

"No," I whispered.

His head hung low, and he pushed his hands even deeper into his pockets.

"This . . . isn't possible." I hugged my arms across my chest. My stomach churned.

"It does feel pretty unreal."

"How?"

A bewildered smile tugged at one corner of his mouth; it fit beautifully in the dusting of his scruff.

I hated it.

Shaking his head, he said, "I can't even imagine."

I hadn't figured out how to close my mouth yet. It just hung open, weighed down by the sickening coincidence.

He shivered once. "I'm sorry I didn't warn you at the clinic—"

"You knew at the clinic?" I asked in a weak voice.

"Kinda." He squinted at the gray sky. "I saw the back of your head before work this morning, but then . . . I didn't think it was *you*."

I gingerly brushed my fingertips under my hair. "The back of my head?"

"It hasn't changed."

"That's a strange thing to say."

His chest sank with a heavy sigh, and he shivered again. "Yeah."

"It's freezing out here, why aren't you in your car?"

He pulled his right hand from his pocket and pointed.

I looked over my shoulder again. Hanging from the seam of the door just below the knob was the loop of a burgundy lanyard.

"I was heading back out, and they swung behind me," he answered without me asking.

"That is so fucked up."

His laugh sputtered, more of a cough. A bodily function he couldn't control.

I snorted. One corner of my lip pulled upward but I forced it back into place. "What are you gonna do?"

"I've called a couple of friends, but I haven't heard back." His shivering wasn't sporadic anymore, but a constant tremor. "You don't happen to have a ladder in your place?"

My expression was enough of an answer for him.

Chuckling, he nodded. "I didn't figure you would. Mine is locked in the shed."

"You have an open window?"

"Yeah the kitchen one under the carport is unlocked. It's just gonna be a pain in the ass to get up to it."

"Is it the same size as the one on my side?"

"Yeah."

"Remi," I scoffed. "Even if you got up to it, you'd never fit in that thing."

"It'd be tight, but I could do it."

"Maybe if you dislocated both of your shoulders."

The smile that spread across his face was too much for the situation, too big for all this wide-open space to contain. Too overwhelming for my system to know what to do with.

"It doesn't matter, anyway. You don't have a ladder, and I can't get to mine. I'm sure one of my friends will get back to me soon."

I chewed on my bottom lip and glanced toward my open door.

"You don't have to invite me in," he said as if the prospect was as traumatizing to him as it was to me.

Behind him a line of near black chased after the sunlight across the sky. Pulling my coat tight around me, I pointed out, "The sun is setting. It's cold out here, and it's gonna keep getting colder. You don't even have a coat on."

"I'm fine. I promise to knock on your door before I lose any fingers or toes."

I forced myself to look up at his face. His thick eyebrows flicked upward, and he met my gaze. His lips pursed slightly, the way they did when he was thinking. Not for the first time, I wished I could read his mind.

Jerking my head to the door I'd left open behind me, I took a step backward. "I'm gonna go inside."

"Good."

I was half-turned away from him, when he spoke again. "Leese, I'm sorry I scared you."

The apology fell from his lips like it cost him nothing and froze me like a deer in headlights. There had been a vast list of sorrys I'd wanted from this man, but they never came. Then there was this one that he just gave away. What was I supposed to do with it?

"Um . . . I'm sorry I yelled at you."

"Thanks." He jerked his chin toward my rental. "Get inside. I'll be okay."

In the quiet and warmth of the indoors, I took my coat off and threw it on one of the kitchen table chairs. And I ignored the little voice remarking about how unsafe it was to leave him out there like that. He said he'd be fine.

But will he?

"Damn it," I hissed.

Chapter Seven

Remi

I wiggled my toes inside of my boots, attempting to gauge how close I was to losing one of them. It had only been awhile since I locked myself out, and I had at least twenty more minutes before I'd knock on Alicia's door. Pulling my phone from my pocket, I sent out yet another text to everyone I knew in this town asking for someone to take me to Ol' Mr. Miller's house to grab a spare key or bring me a ladder—at this point I'd be happy if someone would just let me sit in their warm car for a few minutes. Today had been an emotional roller coaster that deserved a hard drink or two to put it to rest.

Debating if I should jog to town, I wondered if it would keep me from dying of hypothermia.

Alicia's door had only been closed for about a minute before it opened again. And there she was all flesh and bone standing in front of me and stopping my heart at just the sight of her. Her hair was pulled into a ponytail that swung around her shoulders as she spoke. And her amber-colored eyes pinned me like an insect to a board. My memory had at once inflated her vibrancy and came nowhere near it at the same time.

Recovering from the day would be impossible.

"Can you boost me?" she asked, her shoulders back.

It took too much of my focus not to glance down at the way the V-neck of her sweater dropped between her breasts to comprehend what she had just said. Distractingly beautiful tits.

"Can you boost me to the window?"

Initially, I wanted to argue and tell her she didn't have to, but I was a little concerned about frostbite. My nervous system had been shocked so many times in the past few hours, what was one more traumatic event. It's not like I'd be touching her. She might place her hands on my shoulders for a few seconds, but I'd just be holding her shoe.

Accepting defeat from the worst day, I said, "I mean, yeah."

"Okay, let's go." She took the stairs down from the porch leading the way to my carport. The sway of her hips as she walked was a familiar rhythm, and her jeans clung to her hips and ass in a way that *really* worked. It was impossible to keep from overlaying the Alicia I used to know with this new Alicia. The way she had changed might not have been my preference when I was twenty-eight, but I'd be goddamned if it wasn't now.

In the first stroke of good luck I'd had in the past twenty-four hours, I looked up from her ass just before she turned around.

"That one?" She pointed toward the window, and she had a point that I probably wouldn't have fit.

My teeth clattered together despite how I tried to stop it. "Yeah."

"Oh my God, Rem, you would have died out here instead of just knocking on my door."

"No, it's just gotten worse in the past couple of minutes." I moved around her to swing my hand up to break a hole into the screen covering the glass. When I turned, she was running her hands up and down her arms, fighting a losing battle against Michigan winter. "You don't even have a coat on at this point."

"And I have a better understanding of how bad it was for me to leave you out here."

"But you didn't. Come on, you're starting to shiver. I don't like this." I presented my entwined fingers for her to step in. "I've got you, Alicia."

I'd spoken her name innumerable times over the years, but it felt new in my mouth.

Her eyes flicked to mine, but I couldn't see past the steel wall she'd built between us for me to filter out any of her thoughts. Not like when we were at the clinic and her emotions flashed across her face completely unguarded—anger, accusation, affection. Each one had hit me like a physical blow.

"So, I just—" She lifted her hands within a foot of my shoulders and dropped them.

I swallowed, and heat rose up my neck and cheeks. I bent at the knees to make it easier for her to place her foot. My voice came out strained. "Just step there and grab my shoulders for balance."

"Right."

Neither of us moved. I waited for the pressure of her fingers, but when they didn't come I glanced at her face and this time her apprehension was right there.

"Come closer."

She shuffled forward her hands still hovered a few inches too far away.

Straightening to my full height, I got a better grasp of just how close we were standing. There was a crease between her eyebrows, and her lips were pinched in a tight line. Burying my hands back in my pockets to resist running a hand down her arm, I said, "You don't have to do this. If you'll just lend me a blanket, I'll be fine."

She closed her eyes and breathed out a steamy breath. "No, that's silly. Let's just do this."

"You sure?"

"Mmhmm." She cut me off when I opened my mouth to argue. "Get back down there, Rem."

I went back into my lowered position; this time she moved close enough that I could smell something clove scented from her stomach.

Her hands lingered above me for just a moment, before she took hold and placed an ice- and dirt-covered sole of her boot in the cradle of my fingers.

"You ready?" I asked, with a raspy voice.

"Sure."

When I stood, I expected to bear her weight, but instead she bent her knee keeping her opposite leg on the ground. Her arms circled my neck and the scruff on my cheek scraped against the soft skin of her chest. The clove scent was stronger there between the full swells of her breasts.

If my dick twitched, I wasn't really to blame. Our chemistry had never been an issue, and I'd been in a dry spell for a while.

She let go of me as if she'd discovered she was holding a porcupine. "Sorry, I thought I was ready."

"It's okay," I said, I was about to suggest the blanket again, and I was beginning to think that she should take me up on it.

Before I could say anything, she fixed a determined gaze with mine. "I'll be ready this time."

"Third times the charm?"

"Definitely."

We found our positions again, counted to three before I extended her weight in my hands. I had my back against the siding to keep stable while she pushed at the window inching it up with her palms until she could fit her fingers under it. Between my fingers being a little numb and the ice melting from her boots, when she gave one good heave my grasp slipped. She let out a little scream that put my heart in my throat. I wrapped my arms around her thighs hugging her to my chest and my hand squeezed into the flesh of her right ass cheek. Her hands were back at my shoulders holding so tightly her nails bit at my skin through my Henley.

After a few beats, I asked, "Are you okay?"

"I'm fine." One hand at a time, she let go of me and pulled closer to the building. "Can you hoist me up again? The window's open."

It happened in stages, her inching higher until she had a knee placed on either side of my head and I did my best to keep my face from the heat between her thighs. Every inch of her felt too good. She smelled too good. The whole thing was bringing back great memories. The flashbacks settled some when she placed a boot on my shoulder and pushed the rest of the way through the window.

"I'm in," she exclaimed. I could hear the smile in her voice.

"You're amazing," I called back before jogging up my front porch stairs. I only had to wait outside another few seconds before she opened the door—just like every moment I'd laid eyes on her that day, I wasn't prepared.

The grin on her face froze before slipping away, I could feel mine doing the same. My body carried a memory of her weight in my arms, the way my hand sank into her jean covered flesh, her spiced scent still lingered in my nose.

Scrubbing a palm along my jaw, I leaned back on my heels giving her space to exit the threshold. "Thanks."

"You're welcome." She ducked past me hurrying to her door. "I might have scared one of the lives out of your cat."

Running a hand through my hair, I gripped the back of my neck. "She's jumpy, but she'll be okay."

I bent to retrieve my keys. When they'd gotten stuck inside, I'd been heading to Benji's Place for a beer and a burger. But now I wanted a hot shower and whatever I had in the fridge.

Alicia and I paused for just a moment outside of our places assessing the nearness, the few feet and years that separated us.

"Good night."

"Night."

I closed my door behind me and took a step, hearing her echoing step creak on the floorboard just on the other side of the wall. One single, poorly insulated wall.

Chapter Eight

Alicia

I had my coat zipped all the way. With my hood up, I had to turn my head like Batman to see from side-to-side. Everything was quiet now that I'd stopped trudging and crunching my way to what might have been the middle of the wetland.

Little piles of snow weighed down bent blades of sepia-toned grass. A cardinal hopped from the limb of one tree to the next, its light-weight body supported on a thin twig. There were bunny and deer tracks in trails all over the ground. My boot prints were the only signs of humanity on the otherwise undisturbed earth. And that was only what I could see. Then there was the plant life diversity. Every element of this marsh worked together to serve our planet for possibly as far back as twelve thousand years.

These acres of land were being used in exactly the way they needed to be. It would continue that way, only if we were able to save it.

If *I* was able to save it.

"No pressure," I mumbled.

Turning, I started back for the road where my car was parked. Ready to begin the task I was here to do.

The head librarian, Mrs. Simons, had been more welcoming than Deb Creger at Town Hall. Wrinkles deepened around Deb's pinched lips with every sentence I spoke, her gray eyes narrowing at my leaflets and charts.

But I'd dealt with skeptical locals before. I could handle a wary town clerk. I wouldn't move everyone to my side, but I'd try.

"My firm was planning to have the marsh purchased by one of our benefactors when it went to public auction. Our plan was to place protective covenants on the deed. But when it didn't go to auction, we looked into it and found that there was already a development proposal," I explained.

"Why is the protection important?" she asked, skimming over the papers on her desk.

One corner of my mouth lifted. "Oh my goodness, I will try to not get *too* passionate about wetlands."

Some of the tightness relaxed from her expression.

I took it as encouragement to lean into my most earnest self. "I am of the mindset that *all* wetlands should be protected, and Michigan as a state has been protecting them since the late 70s. But that doesn't mean that we aren't still losing them to development and such. Wetlands home such a vast collection of species—both in plant life and animal life, as well as being water filtration powerhouses. Being this close to Lake Michigan, it makes the role this chunk of earth is providing that much more important."

Her scowl was slowly thawing.

"We are *so* lucky here in Michigan," I continued. "Being surrounded by such a significant percentage of the earth's freshwater supply, but that also means that we need to be good stewards of that water and protect it."

"But you're from Chicago," she said.

"I live there, but I grew up just outside of Mackinaw."

Her eyebrows lifted. She assessed me with fresh eyes, a part of the tribe.

"So, not only do I know how important the lake is to the planet, but to people living right here. It's a source of community and fun, but also *tourism*." I gestured to the stack of pamphlets offering tours and attractions next to her desk.

She nodded. "It's our primary industry."

"It is for my hometown too."

"What do they want to build?"

"A resort, with a golf course and little amusement park, and as a tourist location, I think that's great. I even sent them a couple of properties currently listed to consider moving their plans to. Each of those is currently owned by a resident of the area and would benefit someone here directly."

Deb tapped on the map spread out on her desk. "Why here then?"

At this point in the conversation, I had to be very careful. I lowered my voice, leaning close enough to smell her peony-scented perfume. "All I'm allowed to say is that it does not appear to be selling at market value."

She tilted her head and considered everything. "That's state land."

"It is."

"Why would the state sell the land at a discount?"

Internally, I screamed, *Because the developer is the son of a state congressman!*

Externally, I stated, "Legally, I have said all I'm allowed to say."

I didn't know exactly what she inferred to make her sit back in her chair assessing me and the information I had provided. Maybe it was that a stranger with money was coming to take advantage of the area and its people. Maybe it was a general blue-collar distrust of "the man." But there it was. Deb had just moved over to my side. Her jaw set determinedly, and her shoulders squared. She might not *know* why the land was being sold for cheap, but she knew it was an underhanded deal that did not benefit her friends and neighbors.

"So, anyway"—I kept my voice even despite the thrill of victory—"that's why I'm here. Not to stop the development, my firm and I see how it could enrich the county, but to inform the community that its location should be changed."

"Hmm, my son would agree." Again, she tapped the map, this time on a neighboring property. "That's his therapy stables."

I rested my chin on my hand. "Oh, you're the same Cregers."

"We are."

"Is he a therapist?"

"His friend Missy is. She moved back a few years back and convinced Emmett to expand from boarding. Now, equestrian therapy is all they do."

"That's wonderful."

Deb folded her hands on her desk and nodded. "Well, he's gonna want to hear all of this. Let me introduce you."

"That'd be amazing. I was planning to talk to all the neighboring landowners. An introduction to your son would be so helpful."

"Can you meet me there at four-thirty?"

I checked my watch. Furgie needed to be let out beforehand, but it was possible. "I can. Thank you so much, Mrs. Creger."

"Deb, please."

I pressed a hand to my chest. "Alicia."

"Do you play euchre?"

My brain screeched like a record, skipping at the change in subject. "Yeah, of course."

She gave a decided jerk of her head. "You'll have to come to a euchre club meeting with me."

"Euchre club?"

"Yeah, it's just a bunch of us ladies playing cards and chatting. But it still beats the Internet in spreading information."

"Sounds perfect."

Leaving my new buddy, I smiled and waved over my shoulder. As I walked out of the building, I tugged my white, knitted cap lower over my ears. My boots crunched on the frozen sidewalks. I scanned for patches of ice while nearly running to take shelter in the mildly warmer cab of my car.

The air blasted cold through my vents after I turned the key in the ignition. I took a couple of seconds to map out my destinations from Town Hall to my place, and then to the Creger stables. I had roughly twenty minutes to let my dog out and be there on time. Putting the car in drive, I made tracks.

In a robotic voice, my car read Sadie's text aloud. *Any new ex-husband sightings?*

I sent back the longer text dictating to my car. *Fortunately, no, but I'm heading home now. And you know, we share a wall! But honestly, it's been a couple of days, and I feel a little more rational about it. Now that the shock has passed.* It had been four days since running into Remi—and kinda sorta climbing him like a literal tree. I was definitely not over it. I braced myself for impact every time I left my rental or got back to it. So far, the only time I'd seen him was the day after, when he was wearing scrubs with a tuxedo design and a little bowtie around his neck on his way to his mailbox.

"What is going on with you, Remi?" I asked from the safety of my half of the duplex.

But otherwise, he was gone a lot. And so was I. Avoiding him was easier than I thought it would be.

> Me: I have been hella productive because of it though. I'm gonna save these wetlands and get back to Chicago.

> Sadie: That's right you are! And hurry cause I miss you! How's our little Furg?

I could practically see the pout that would be on Sadie's face if I were talking to her in person.

> Me: She's doing all right. I'll keep you posted, but I'm sure the antibiotics are helping. What about you? Anything interesting going on there?

There was a pause as I turned onto the dirt road leading to my duplex. When Remi's empty carport came into view, I exhaled the breath I didn't realize I was holding.

> Sadie: Don't be mad.

"God damn it." I groaned and squeezed the steering wheel so tight the leather creaked under my grip.

> Me: Tell me it's not fuckboy.

> Sadie: It is fuckboy.

> Me: Why??????

Putting my car in park, I snatched my phone from my purse and hit dial.

She answered, "I have a very unfortunate type."

"If you wanna fuck a fuckboy, then go for it, but you can't want to date a fuckboy."

This man had caused my friend a couple of teary nights drinking red wine and watching *Pride and Prejudice*—both the 2005 and the BBC versions. He was a spectacular lawyer at our firm, as well as a spectacular dipshit with my bestie's heart. She just couldn't stop falling back into his bed.

Watching the pattern repeat itself broke my heart by proxy.

But then, one of my favorite things about Sadie was her forgiving heart. So I put a lot of blame on lawyer, fuckboy-extraordinaire. He could just stop messing with her.

"I don't want to date him . . . I just . . . God, he's sweet when it's just the two of us, and I like it." She groaned.

"Yeah, but he's just full of bullshit, and that's how he gets you."

"I know. I need you to hurry up and get back here because I listen to you better than I do myself."

"You want to see the best in everyone." I opened the side door to Furgie wagging the back half of her body and whining. "Hi, sweet pea!"

"Aw, I can hear her being adorable."

"She is too. She's feeling so much better. Remi did a good job."

"You said that."

"He made her feel comfortable during the visit too. I'm not surprised he's good at this." It was a challenge to clip the leash to Furgie's collar with her excited wiggling.

"No one is all bad, right?"

"He wasn't bad. We were just"—I struggled to find the word I wanted while I chose not to look to deeply into my knee-jerk reaction to defend him—"dumb. Anyway, I don't even know why I brought him up. Can we go back to talking about you?"

She huffed. "Sure."

"So, what happened?"

"He was at the office Friday, and he was gorgeous and flirty, and now he's texting—"

"Have you agreed to go out to dinner with him?"

"Dinner?" she scoffed. "You mean drinks? No, he hasn't asked."

"What are you gonna do if he does?"

Furgie hopped from the shoveled walk to the snow-covered yard.

"I don't know," Sadie answered.

I exhaled a puff of steam, wondering how best to proceed. "I know you want to believe that he can change—that you see a lot of good in him. But even if he did, could you trust it at this point? After the highs and lows he's put you through."

"Probably not."

I hated how deflated she sounded.

"You know you are deserving of a hot man to be totally into, right? And you deserve for that hot man to be totally excited about you too."

"I know. I'll stop texting him."

"I think it's for the best."

"I think we just accelerated my *Pride and Prejudice* night."

"Let's stream it together tonight. My Wi-Fi is working because of you."

Her voice brightened a bit. "I'd like that."

A few minutes later, I put Furgie inside after running around with her. I snatched a granola bar out of the cupboard.

Around a mouthful of food, I mumbled on my way out the door, "I'm sorry, Furg, I'll be home as soon as I can. But I have to go."

She gave me the saddest brown eyes as the latch clicked into place.

Still feeling guilty, I hopped back into my car and started following the directions to the stables. When the cellular connection sputtered out, I was grateful I'd snapped a screenshot of the directions. Ten minutes later, I arrived following the plowed winding driveway until a large barn and stable came into view. Behind it sat a house with a high-pitched roof.

"Shoot. Nice digs here, Mr. Creger," I said to no one.

I wasn't sure where to go, but there were a number of older model cars, all of them rather rusted. As well as two or three newer ones. One of them could be Deb's—she might already be inside a building.

Glancing at my watch, I confirmed that I was only two minutes early. I zipped my coat to my chin and stepped out into the cold following the trail of packed snow to the empty stable. The smell of livestock was strong in the warm building. It wasn't overwhelming, just present. One of those details of rural living I'd forgotten in the past couple of years of city life. I continued through the open door at the other end to the large barn. A sliding door was open enough for a horse to walk through, it gently banged into the building over and over catching on the wind.

Inside, there was a collection of teens in helmets sitting atop their mounts, and a man with shaggy dark hair peaking from under his helmet. He sat ramrod straight.

There was one other man, and the sight of him set my nervous system into overdrive instantly—my stomach dropped, my palms went clammy, and my cheeks heated.

Once again, I was unexpectedly in the same place as Remi in a long-sleeve T-shirt clinging to his biceps and chest. His thighs strained against his dark blue pants that were practically painted on. They probably served a purpose for horseback riding, but when he stood in the stirrups they were . . . There was nothing left to the imagination.

Not that I needed to use my imagination. I'd seen his ass before.

Not that I was thinking about it.

But it was right there and . . . sculpted.

The reins hung from his easy grip, and I felt an echo of it on my upper thigh. He rode a gray speckled horse from one jump to another, his body following the movement with confidence and a grace that belied his large frame. But this time, I wasn't caught completely off-guard, and I took control over the bombardment of emotions and stress at just the sight of him. I could even detach enough from my feelings to enjoy how he'd filled out over the past couple of years. Everything about him was broader—his shoulders, chest, abdomen.

It was rude how well he sat a horse. It wasn't a skill I found particularly hot, but there was something annoyingly romantic about a man in a saddle.

Obviously, I still struggled with his presence, but at least now I was more prepared to encounter this man who had only gotten unfairly fucking hotter in the intervening years. The same way I could mentally prepare to encounter a flu shot.

Quietly, I insisted that it was perfectly safe for me to acknowledge all of this. I could appreciate him from afar, the way I would any man. But he wasn't just *any man*. And while it was undeniable that I was attracted to him, it wasn't entirely safe either.

Rude.

Fucking Rude.

Chapter Nine

Remi

"Alicia," Deb called above the arena.

My grip on Stone's reins tightened like I was holding on for dear life. The horse had already launched for our last jump in the demonstration. Every muscle in my body grew rigid mid-air. I didn't have time to correct or even regret how the impact was going to crash through my joints before Stone's front hooves landed in the dirt. My vertebrae compacted causing my ears to ring as sand splattered across my face.

I kept my seat, but just barely.

From the catwalk overhead, Emmett groaned. "Oof."

Brooks' usually placid expression flinched, his eyebrows shot up and his mouth twisted.

"You okay, Mr. Akerman?" Conner, a scrawny sophomore, half-stood in his stirrups. His voice pitched, carrying both shock and concern.

I rolled my head from shoulder-to-shoulder, testing just how sore I was going to be tomorrow. "Yeah, so that looked as bad as it felt, huh?"

"It looked really bad."

Positioning Stone so I couldn't check if Alicia saw or not, I forced my voice to remain casual. "Try to not do what I did. Conner, why don't you go first?"

In the past few days my mind had wandered a familiar path, no matter how hard I tried not to. The memory of bearing her weight—her fullness filling my hands. It was more to do with how long it had been since I'd been with anyone, and less to do with her body in my arms. If she was any other woman, I would have been just as preoccupied—definitely less traumatized by the encounter—and I would have tried for second or third.

He side-eyed the course, jumps were not his favorite activity, but it was what we were working on this week. After a few more seconds, I opened my mouth to offer for someone else to go when he urged his horse into a trot.

Brooks guided his mare to stand next to me and Stone. "That's her?"

"Nora told you?" I asked, even though I knew the answer.

He shrugged a shoulder in response.

"That's her."

Almost against my will, I looked over my shoulder to find Alicia climbing the stairs to the second story where Missy's office had been added a few years ago. Emmett and his mom, Deb, waited for Alicia with their elbows propped on the railing of the catwalk. She pulled her bright hair over one shoulder, her smile beaming. She could wield her charm like a weapon; at least she was using it for good. The rumor network had spread about the gorgeous redhead who'd just moved to town to stop a resort development from murdering turtles, or maybe they were cutting down every last tree in a hundred-mile radius. Or no, it was mining the dunes off the lake and burying the county under Lake Michigan.

It depended on who relayed the information. There was even a version of the story where she was a nosy meddler who wanted to stop economic growth at all cost.

Alicia stood just outside of the door Emmett held open for her. I felt her pause like we were balanced on a narrow edge, and the turn of her head toward me could shove us both over. Send us falling, plummeting, toward . . . somewhere. Who knew? The moment her gaze caught mine, tectonic plates shifted beneath me—their vibrations quaking through my chest.

One corner of my mouth twitched up, and I raised my hand in a wave.

She tilted her head to one shoulder and waved back.

Then she disappeared into the office, and it was over. Everything was okay. Nothing catastrophic.

We remained whole.

Toward the end of our marriage, we couldn't stop hurting each other, as if the pain was the only connection we had left. The last thing I could do for her as we tore our lives apart. The only way I could get her eyes on me. The only way I could see her.

Otherwise, we were ghosts haunting the same space while desperation consumed me—willing to go to new lows just for a glimpse.

I'd never hurt her like that again. I'd never hurt anyone like that again. It was a small consolation.

"Crazy she's here in this town," Brooks said, watching as the next student started the jump course. It was more his responsibility than mine as the head coach of the high school's equestrian team. I was acting as assistant, but I was really more of a warm body than anything else.

"You have no idea."

"Hmm?"

"She rented the other half of the duplex."

His face remained expressionless as usual, but he turned his head to meet my gaze. "No shit."

I inhaled deeply, preparing to relay the story of being locked out for the first time. Up until that moment, I hadn't felt any desire to speak about that evening. But my feelings had untangled some over the past few days, and possibly more importantly, Brooks barely spoke in general. There was no way he'd willingly tell anyone else. It wasn't that any of it was a secret, but it was private in a way.

The saddle creaked under Brooks as he leaned back, taking in the last of my tale. "You good?"

"Yeah, man—"I cut myself off and reconsidered. "Honestly, I don't know."

I ran a hand down Stone's neck, her soft coat under my palm and the coarse hair of her mane against my knuckles. In the silence, I wondered if I'd said too much. Brooks and I had never talked like this. He was my friend, even a good friend, but he was a "let's sit quietly in the same group" kind of guy. He didn't ask for much, but he didn't give a lot either. I wasn't equipped to differentiate if I'd pushed him out of his comfort zone.

I was about to make an excuse to ride away when he finally spoke. "What can you make right?"

"Huh?"

"Did you ever think you'd see her again?"

It was hard to process his question when I was in shock at hearing him string so many words together. "No."

He tugged at the strap clipped under his chin tilting his head back, looking away like eye contact was a burden. "Seems like an unexpected opportunity to make something right by her."

My hand slipped from the saddle's cantle to my thigh as his suggestion sank in. He rode away, leaving me to the wrestle with this new idea he'd just planted, and the weeds sprouting up around it.

Chapter Ten

Alicia

T here was nothing to eat in my apartment, still. For the past week I'd lived off of take-out, granola bars, and the limited supplies I could get from the party store, and it'd carried me through so far. But if I didn't get some real fruits and vegetables in the house soon I was going to contract scurvy or something. Driving twenty minutes to the nearest Meijer after a long day of meeting locals and getting signatures on my petition—as well as rejections—was something I couldn't bring myself to do. Starting on-location jobs while not having my friends near to help recharge my battery was always the hardest part. It made for nights feeling overly drained.

I wandered the produce section of the locally owned grocery store. It could have been built anywhere between 1975 and 1990, and they hadn't updated it since, keeping with a dark brown and forest green color pallet. Options were limited, but compared to the party store, it was a practical smorgasbord. A cucumber and some carrots rolled around in my cart, as I considered which three of the dozen apples were best. I did a voice command through my earbuds to call Sadie. It was unlikely she'd answer, but I could leave her a voicemail anyway. I was distracted by her recorded greeting as the ancient automatic front doors opened.

"Hey Mr. Akerman," a teenage cashier greeted.

"Oh shit," I hissed, dropping to crouch on the grimy tile floor, hidden behind the apples.

"Hey, Conner," Remi replied, unaware of my presence. "How are you doin'?"

"Good. Slow night. Just kinda waiting for close."

"Yeah, I get that."

I chewed on my lower lip, unsure of what I should do next. I could stay down there for a little while, maybe Remi needed toilet paper or something and he'd walk in the other direction, then I could make a quick escape and accept my future with scurvy. I'd had great luck so far avoiding him. Zero run-ins since the stable a few days ago. It was more annoying than traumatizing to recall because of the way his pants hugged his ass.

"I'll just stay down here, and he'll go away," I whispered.

Rolling my eyes, I remembered how I'd thought he couldn't surprise me because I knew he was in the town. "Idiot."

In the wait for the coast to clear, I lost track of where he'd gone. The store was mostly empty; the only sound was the HVAC system and The Roxette's "It Must Have Been Love" playing through the overhead speakers.

"He's gotta be gone—"

"'Licia?" His voice came from behind me.

With a scream, I threw the apples I'd had clutched to my chest in the air and whipped around.

One of the them landed on his shoulder more than him actually catching it, the other two thudded to the tile floor.

He took a big step back. "Woah."

Heat rose up my neck, and I retrieved one of the apples from under the produce stand to give myself a second to hide. I would have preferred making a total fool of myself in front of one hundred people instead of just him.

"Don't sneak up on me," I said from under the stand on my hands and knees. But even as I said it, it felt unfair.

"I didn't mean to."

Coming to a crouch, I looked up at him. From this angle, he appeared about ten feet tall and even broader than usual. His legs were clad in navy scrub pants, and his corduroy coat was zipped to the top. One green apple dwarfed in his big hand at his side.

He offered his free hand to me. "Do you need help up?"

"No."

His arm fell back to his side. Nodding slowly, he chewed on his bottom lip looking around the store then back to me. "What are you doing down there?"

I flung my arms out. "I dropped my apples."

After I hid from you, and you scared the shit out of me.

"Right." Taking another step back, he looked like he was about to flee then decided against it. "How are you settling in?"

I went to answer him but realized how weird it was to continue talking to him from the floor, so I pushed to stand with my hands on my thighs ignoring the crack of one of my knees. From this height, I could make out the dusting of reddish scruff on his jaw. It was an outrage for me to behave like a complete embarrassment while he looked . . . like that.

"Fine." I gripped one of my elbows with my other hand, hoping I looked chill but sure I looked like someone trying to look unaffected. "Um, yeah, it was good to meet the Cregers and Missy the other night. They're gonna help me out. So, that's good."

Remi cleared his throat. "That's great news."

"Yeah."

"How's Furgie doing?"

A genuine smile spread across my face. "She's a lot better. Thank you."

"That's grews." A crease formed between his eyebrows as he blinked.

I snorted, my cheeks beginning to burn from secondhand embarrassment—which was a bold feeling considering he'd just found me hiding from him. "You mean, great news?"

"Yeah." He sighed. "But I'd already said it, so I tried to say something different."

"I think it's grews too."

He laughed and even the fluorescent lights couldn't diminish his handsomeness. My stomach flipped. I always did love his laugh. It was full, and from the gut. It was even better when I was the one making it happen.

"Anyway, I've gotta get home to her," I said. Taking hold of my cart's handle, I tried to pretend like all I wanted from the store were the three items inside of it.

"Of course. I'm sure I'll see you around."

I scoffed. "I'm sure."

He took a few steps away, and I grabbed whatever looked even remotely appetizing and nutritious on the way to the cashier. It was when I was placing my floor apple, a cucumber, carrots, a giant bag of trail mix, and beef jerky that I realized I'd been recording a voicemail for Sadie the whole time.

"Oh, holy hell," I mumbled. "Well, I guess you'll call me back to unpack all this."

The teenager ringing me up gave me a skeptical glance but looked away at my forced smile. It felt like time was being pulled through sludge, moving at an unnaturally slow pace while I pretended not to know exactly where Remi was the whole time I waited for my total.

Where was this hyper awareness of his existence a few minutes ago? I demanded, silently.

I had just paid and was leaving the building when my phone started ringing. I answered it knowing who it was without even looking. "Hey . . ."

"So, that voicemail you just left me," Sadie said through the speaker.

"You listened to that already?"

"Uh-huh. I was so confused, what was all of that?"

I slid into the driver's seat of my vehicle. "You know, just that classic situation of spotting your ex at the grocery store, panicking for no reason, hiding behind a pile of apples, and then having him sneak up behind you, anyway."

"Okay, so that was Remi you were talking to?"

"Yes."

After a beat of silence, she asked, "Can I say something truly fucking unnecessary?"

"Why not?"

"Are you sure? Because it's not a helpful observation."

"Lay it on me, lady."

"He sounds hot."

I groaned. "He is."

"Not that it matters."

Letting my head fall back on the headrest, I gritted my teeth. "It does not matter."

Chapter Eleven

Remi

I t had snowed overnight. A fresh blanket of shimmering white covered the ground—smoothing over but not filling the little paw and body prints from Furry Furg. I wondered absently how her rash was doing as I scraped the pavement clean. The vibrations shivered up my forearms in front of Alicia's half of the duplex.

I'd already finished on my half and the snow from my driveway. The thought of stopping there had crossed my mind, but then I'd heard Brooks' question from the other afternoon and decided not to.

It had been just over a week since our lives collided. I was still dealing with the whiplash, but I didn't mind cleaning up snow. The morning sun shone golden light everywhere. My hands were warm inside of my gloves. The physical labor kept my body temperature high enough that I was almost too warm in a sweatshirt and overall snow pants. Under my hat, my hair was damp from exertion. It was productive and satisfying.

I'd finished her walk and was moving on to her driveway when her side door opened. She stood in the doorway blinking at me and the mounds lining the cement path. She wrapped her soft pink bathrobe tighter across her front, fighting back the cold. I wouldn't say that my memories of her body were unwelcome, but they were inconvenient—persistent images flashed through my mind: her soft, hot skin under my palms and her taste on my tongue.

"You don't have to do that. I can shovel my own snow," she said dragging me back to the present.

My stomach flipped at the sound of her voice, but I forced an easy grin at the shovel as I scraped it along the dirt drive. "Hey, Alicia, how are you?"

Her eyeroll was practically audible. With a voice as dry as the air, she remarked, "Hi, Remi, I'm fine. How are you? Some snow we got last night."

Chuckling, I leaned my forearm on the tip of the wooden handle.

Her hair was piled atop her head in a single scrunchie—russet waves cascaded down one side of her face. Warm sunlight illuminated the faint smattering of freckles on the bridge of her nose. Her skin was smooth and creamy, and her lips were a pale rose. In the light, her amber eyes were almost golden.

I scraped the toe of my boot at a patch of ice, needing to look away from her. Her beauty made my chest ache. I remembered this feeling; her loveliness was bad for my health.

"I'm fine, thank you. Just enjoying my morning." I took a fortifying breath before looking at her again. "I know you can shovel your own snow. But I would do this for any neighbor. I don't want to treat you worse than I would treat anyone else. I can stop if you want me to."

She pursed her lips to one side and considered the remaining work to be done before her eyes slid back to me. The glimmer of amusement almost did me in, almost friendly in its comfortability. "I mean . . . if you're enjoying your morning . . ."

I grinned down at the ground.

"And it is such a good workout," she went on. "I wouldn't want to take this healthy exercise away from you."

"So thoughtful."

"I know. I'm practically doing this *for* you."

"Practically."

She lifted a cotton-clad shoulder and turned to go back inside. "Well, that's that then."

If looking at her was bad for my health, not seeing her was worse and panic gripped me. Words tumbled out of my mouth, desperately trying to pull her back. "Tell me about these turtles."

Her giggle sent shivers across my scalp. "Turtles?"

My smile was probably a little bit dopey. It could have been exposure therapy, or how safely domestic the morning felt, but for the first time since seeing her in the exam room at the clinic, her presence didn't feel like a threat. Instead, it seemed that something broken within me could heal—unfinished business put to rest.

"Aren't you here to save turtles?" I asked.

She laughed with her whole body; it pulsed through me with the beat of my heart. Healing, indeed.

"That's hilarious, I love small towns. What a fun little game of telephone," she remarked. "I'm here for the marsh over by Emmett's."

First name basis.

A hook snagged on my brain, a whisper of a feeling I had no right to feel. Suddenly, the conversation felt a little less homey, and my intentions were more questionable.

I pitched my shovel to fill it with a new batch of snow. "Gotcha."

"I haven't checked for a turtle population, but I'm sure I'm saving those too. Did someone mention them? It wouldn't be a bad angle. People love turtles."

"I think one of the high schoolers did the other night at the stables."

Without stopping in my work, I bore the pressure of her considering me. "Do you know the principal at the school?"

"Brock Lewell, yeah he's a decent guy. He let us use the school parking lot for a pop-up vet clinic day last summer."

"That's great. Do you think he'd let me do a water supply presentation?"

I straightened, the handle slipping from my grip remained where it was, held up from the weight in its scoop. "Now that's clever. I bet he would; he'd probably welcome it."

"Fantastic. I'll get that set up. Take care, Rem."

"See ya."

Ten minutes later, by the time I'd finished clearing the snow, I was breathing deep. Frozen breaths and steam floated up from my bare forearms where I'd pushed my sleeves up. I'd filed through the confusing bit of emotions that had arisen from our conversation, placing them back neatly where they belonged. Confirming that, while unexpected, they were harmless.

I was halfway up the drive when I spotted a mug waiting atop a metal stool just outside of Alicia's door.

I sipped it as I went around to my side entrance. The coffee with cream was almost too strong. Acidic and bitter. Just the way I liked it.

Chapter Twelve

Remi

The fire in my wood burning stove cast an orange glow across my television screen. I'd seen this nature documentary a few times already, but the cinematography was beautiful, and the narrator's voice was soothing. My shift at the clinic had been exhausting, and this time would have been better used finishing my charts, but my cat, was curled up on my lap. Her contented purring lulled me into a deep relaxation, weighing down my eyelids.

I was just dosing off when my phone buzzed with a text. It was a video from my best friend, Owen, of his husky, Bandit, burrowing into the snow. White clumps gathered around his head like a mane. But then in the last few seconds of the video, Owen accidentally caught another one of his dogs, Indie, charging at his six-foot fence and then launching himself up it and over to the other side. Off screen Owen exclaimed, "You have to be fucking kidding me."

Chuckling, I typed out a response, half-aware—*maybe sightly more than half*—of Alicia moving on the other side of our shared wall. It wasn't thin enough for me to know exactly what she was doing, but I could determine she was in her kitchen. Her voice came through too muffled to hear, but I assumed she was talking to Furgie—it was a bit higher and sweeter than her normal tone. My lips twitched in something like a smile.

Then all at once, everything went loud. Furgie's bark was like percussions. Something large fell to the floor. But it was Alicia's scream that echoed in my mind. It harmonized with the ringing in my ears. My heart punched against my ribs. Bliss launched from my lap as I stood. I rounded my chair running for my front door. There was more barking, and something else crashed against the wall.

I couldn't breathe.

That terrified sound coming from Alicia had robbed me of everything but my need to get to her. To put my body between her and whatever threat she was facing. Whoever he was, I'd tear him apart with my bare hands. My vision was actually red.

I burst into the pitch-black night, barely any light spilled from our windows. Gripping her doorknob, I turned it. It was locked. It didn't matter. I threw my shoulder against it with all my weight. Splinters of wood flew from the frame as I forced the locked latch open. It hit the wall and swung back at me.

Alicia let out one more scream then fell silent at the sight of me breathing heavily in the shattered remains of her entryway. She was crouched under the countertop, while Furgie barked on the other side of the living room wall.

Every muscle in my body was rigid and flexed. Scanning the apartment, I couldn't see anyone but her. Beside her, I lowered to kneel on the carpet. The urge to touch her, to make sure she was in one piece was a physical thing. It lodged in my throat. But I didn't trust myself to be gentle enough with adrenaline coursing through my blood, so I tilted my head from side-to-side to assess if she'd been hurt.

She stared back at me with her eyes wide and accusing, and her mouth hanging open.

My words scraped through my dry throat. "Is there someone here?"

"Remi," she ground out. Looking past me, she glared. "My door."

"Where is he?"

She blinked refocusing on me. "Who?"

"You screamed."

Understanding dawned on her face, but I still felt very much in the dark. "That's why you broke through my door."

A muscle twitched in my jaw.

"No one's here."

"I'm not following."

An irritated edge remained in the glint of her eyes, but her shoulders relaxed away from her ears. For the barest moment, she pressed her palm to my chest where my heart thrummed. She snatched it back, taking my balance with her—I caught myself with one hand on the carpet. The pressure of contact remained.

"It's a bird," she said.

"A bird?" I repeated.

She rubbed the side of her neck. "Well, a good-sized bird."

"There's no one here?"

"No." She shook her head.

Exhaling through pinched lips, I closed my eyes as gratitude and relief washed through me.

She was safe.

"A bird."

"A good-sized bird," she insisted.

"I can take care of a bird." When I opened my eyes, I found Alicia with her eyebrows raised as high as they could go. "What?"

"Kinda seems like you were here to take care of a whole-ass human."

Without knowing how to respond I just shrugged and ignored the sick feeling in my stomach. Now that I was growing aware of myself again, I was certain that I would have charged to help anyone. But my urgency. The lack of conscious decision on my part deserved self-reflection, but before I could look into it much further, I . . . didn't. Of course I reacted quickly. I was scared for my neighbor—my ex-wife, even.

There was nothing to read into.

"I need a towel," I said.

"For the bird?"

I smirked. "Well, a good-sized towel."

"Smart ass." She peaked over my shoulder in the direction of where Furgie barked and scratched at the wall. Alicia chewed on her bottom lip; she leaned back against the counter.

Tilting my head, I considered her. "I don't think it's going to dive-bomb you."

"You don't *think* so, but you don't *know*."

God, this woman.

"Where's a towel? I'll get it," I offered.

"There should be one in the dryer—" she continued explaining the location, but I was sure it was in the same closet by the side-door as mine was. The stackable washer and dryer were just where I'd expected, behind bi-fold doors. On one of the handles, a bright-green lace bra dangled, and I wondered if she had a matching pair of underwear. She always did like a set.

Unbidden, the image of her wearing only that popped into my mind.

It was an effort to divert my thoughts. Instead, I became singularly attentive in finding a towel. Pulling a big, new looking, fluffy terry cloth out of the dryer, I strode past where Alicia was huddled under the countertop and into the living room. I instantly spotted the bird perched on a curtain rod. Furgie continued jumping underneath it; her claws scraped the wood paneled wall trying to run up it. The black feathers on the bird's breast caught the light with each of its quick breaths. It was pretty worn out, but not so much that it didn't try to fly away as I caught it in the middle of the towel.

"I got it," I called over my shoulder. Furgie whined and bounced around my legs, pulling my attention between the bird and not stepping on the dog as I moved toward the demolished front door.

Standing, Alicia gave the bundle in my hands a weary look. "I hope it likes the opulent absorption of my new towel. I'll probably have to burn it after this."

"I'm sure that's exactly what the bird is thinking, 'Wow, thank God, for the opulence.' "

"And absorption."

It wiggled a bit inside my hands. At the gaping door jam, I almost opened my arms but then thought better of it. "Will you put the leash on Furg? I don't want her chasing after this thing when I let it go."

"Right. Yeah, good idea."

A few moments later, I released the bird into the night with Furgie pulling at Alicia's arm. It flew to the trees lining the property, disappearing into the dark.

After a few seconds, the dog started whining, and Alicia asked, "Will it be okay?"

"It didn't look injured. How'd it get in?"

"I think through the woodburning stove, I don't know, it all happened really fast."

I made a mental note to check the cap was secure at the top of the chimney in the morning. But it would have to come second to fixing her door. Now that I could really assess the damage I'd done—it wasn't going to be the easiest correction to make. I'd destroyed more than just the latch. One of the hinges had torn out of the wall, and another one was barely hanging on. The door frame itself would have to be replaced.

There was no way it was going to be secure enough for her to sleep at her place. If it had been easy for me to break in when it was in perfect working order, it would take a light breeze to bring it down now.

"You really pulled a Kool-Aid Man." She bent and picked up a splinter the length of her hand.

"I did . . ." There was no way to suggest what I needed to that didn't make me into an even bigger asshole, so I just asked, "How do you feel about sleeping at my place tonight?"

Chapter Thirteen

Alicia

T he past couple of minutes had left me flabbergasted, and I wouldn't have thought that it could get more surreal, but then where there's a will apparently Remi will find a way.

With all the enthusiasm that I did not feel, I looked directly at him. "That's gonna be a hard 'no.' "

"There isn't any way to keep anyone out at this point. Let's take a second and look at the situation," he reasoned.

"Second taken, I'm good. I'll be staying here."

Gesturing to the gaping hole in the front of my apartment, he said, "I can't fix this tonight."

"I have cardboard and duct tape; it'll be practically indestructible." I shooed him away with the wave of my hand. "You can go now. Thank you for taking care of the bird, I'm good from here."

He remained planted where he stood. "I fucked your door."

"Well, don't."

"Come on, you know what I'm saying."

"I do, and there's no way that I'm sleeping at your place." I gave him a shove that did nothing to move him. He was . . . very solid. Touching him was like trying to take only one spoonful of my favorite ice cream, it just made me want more—all the more reason for me to do a better job avoiding him and definitely not sleeping anywhere near him. It wasn't like I would backslide into that toxic mess, but I was also only human.

"If it was that easy to break through when it wasn't broken, it'd be nothing now," he pointed out.

"I bet your shoulder is going to hurt like hell tomorrow."

"I can't stress how much I didn't feel anything."

"Aren't you just a big strong man," I deadpanned.

"That's not what I'm saying."

"I'm not safe if the door is perfect. I'll take my chances."

"Alicia, please, if someone gets in here—"

"Who is this person? I haven't noticed a dark crime circuit in the mean streets of Grand Ridge."

"If something happened to you because of me I'd never forgive myself."

"It wouldn't be because of you. It would be because of whoever this terrible person is lurking in the shadows and lying in wait."

He scraped a palm across his mouth. Behind his hand, I knew that his jaw was clenched by the way his eyes pierced me, these tell-tail signs of barely restrained irritation. My guard snapped back into place, ready to rise above whatever shitty thing he was about to do or say.

Instead, he pulled in a deep breath and visibly forced himself to relax. "Just take mercy on me. You saw what I did when it was just a bird."

"Bit of an overreaction, BTW."

"Probably, but you sounded like you needed me—help." He corrected quickly, but his first sentence still hung there pushing us both off-center. "Please, Leese, put on your pj's and I'll change my sheets. You can have my bed. I won't even talk to you if you want that."

Bad idea.

I couldn't really put my finger on *why*, but it was. Probably. It could also be just fine.

Yes, we had treated each other terribly. But that had been years ago, I'd grown and gone to therapy. He couldn't hurt me like he used to, and I was a little curious to see who he'd become while I was away. Who was this Remi who broke down doors, captured and released birds, shoveled his neighbor's walk, and took care of sick animals? Who was this man who despite all the ways I damaged him years ago would still rather have me spend the night in his bed alone than risk me getting hurt?

Furgie placed her front paws on my calf, and I bent to scratch her head happy for the excuse to avoid looking at him.

"So many more birds are gonna get in," he said.

Shithead.

I couldn't fight back a little smile. "I can't believe I'm going to do this."

"You will," his voice carried more relief than was entirely reasonable.

"For just tonight."

"Great, thank you."

Cutting my gaze up to him, I added, "I will decide if we're speaking or not when I get there."

The smile he gave me was a bit too knowing for my taste, but I found myself *wanting* to smile back.

"I might not," I insisted.

"Where's that cardboard and duct tape, I'll get this as good as it can get."

Furgie remained on her leash when we got to Remi's a few minutes later; he wanted to see how she'd behave around his cat before giving her free rein of the space. He held the door for us to enter, Furgie's nose investigating the smells on the air, and me in my joggers and a sweatshirt. The kitchen and the window I climbed through was to my right, and unlike my first time being in his space, I didn't avoid taking in the details of his home.

It had the same dated interior and appliances as my half, with some improvements. Four pots hung over the sink from a simple rack, and the blinds were nicer than the cheapest option the store offered that were at my place. I recognized the quilt that his grandma made and gave him for his high school graduation, folded and hanging off the arm of the sofa. I wanted to run my fingers over it, to find the little stitch imperfections that I used to fidget with when it was draped across my lap. It was the coziest thing I'd ever "owned"—I'd never found another blanket to replace it despite how much I tried.

I was surprised how many photos hung in frames on the walls, most of them contained people that I recognized, his family and such. There was one of him and Owen—time had been good to that man—on the beach. There was a group photo of the staff at the vet clinic sitting on what I assumed was a bar patio. A string of warm-colored globe lights were strung overhead and lit their smiling faces. Hazel, who I remembered from Remi's time in vet school, sat next to the receptionist, Nora. There was a second man sitting next to Remi who I couldn't quite place. It didn't matter anyway, because I was too busy taking in the light-hearted grin on Remi's face. It was more than happiness alight in his expression. He was confident and completely at ease.

I didn't ruin him.

With more than a little relief, I sighed. He was more than *okay*.

"Lots of smells, huh, Furg?" He crouched to scratch her face in both of his large hands.

"I like your pictures," I said.

"Yeah, thanks. I put a bunch up when I was in Pheonix—my therapist thought it'd make me feel more connected. When I moved I put them all back up and added some more over the years."

"You have a therapist?"

It wasn't an easy image to reconcile, the man I knew talking to a stranger, possibly crying in front of a them. He never would have when we were married, he hadn't been willing when I'd asked. But then I'd waited too long to ask. The papers that sealed our fate, our division, clutched in my hands.

"Yes, but we stopped regular sessions a few months ago."

I scoffed. "Great timing with me moving in next door and all of that."

"Tell me about it." He laughed. "No, I'm good. I'm surprised how good, actually."

The comment was off handed; it wasn't meant to inflict any pain. I was sure of it. But it did. I almost said a shitty comment about being happy he was so unaffected by me but stopped myself just in time. My reaction to cut him for an unintentional pain unsettled me. Especially, when there was truth to what he'd said, seeing him caused me so many feelings, most of them were confusing, but a great many of them were . . . good.

"I'm surprised too." Needing to look away, I spotted a photo of a young toddler on the fridge. "Is that Maisey?"

Reaching for the image, he plucked it from underneath the magnet. "Yeah. I took it when I visited for Christmas this year."

He'd clearly caught her mid-giggling fit, the smile on her face was so big, I couldn't help but smile back. She had big gray eyes, and blond curls ending around her jaw, and a onesie on that read, *I'm Santa's Favorite*.

"She's a cutie," I said, not just because it was polite—she was actually cute.

The affection in his eyes and his little lopsided grin as he considered his niece almost didn't hurt at all. I was almost entirely happy for him, which felt like progress.

"She is. She's a little charmer." Putting the photo back, he added, "She reminds me of you, actually."

"*Me?*"

"She has that same effortless charm that you have, people just lean toward her when she's in a room."

My cheeks were beginning to warm, and it wasn't from the embers dying in the woodburning stove. "She's a *baby*, everyone is charmed by babies."

"Not everyone. And yeah, I'm her uncle, and I think she's the best baby to ever be a baby, but it's more than that. She's magnetic. She's got this genuine soul."

With my gaze dropping to the floor, I tucked my hair behind my ears. "Does her maturity level remind you of me too?"

He snorted. "No. She would never scream at a bird."

"It was a good-sized bird."

"Repeating that doesn't make it true."

"So now you're the bird expert?"

"I kinda have a degree in it."

"You have a degree in *birds*?"

"My textbooks mentioned them." He moved into the living room as Furgie and I trailed behind. "Want me to get the fire going again or are you going off to bed?"

"Is it your bedtime?"

"No, I'll be up for a couple of hours."

I noticed what he was offering for what it was, it was barely late evening, definitely before I would normally go to bed. But he was giving me the option to retreat, and gain distance.

I shook my head. "I'm not tired."

"You hungry?"

"Not really, but I could snack."

He moved toward the kitchen, and despite how he squeezed past me trying not to enter my space, his arm brushed mine. Even though it wasn't even skin on skin, my stomach flipped, and my heart skipped a beat or two. Nothing I couldn't ignore.

But then his back was turned to me, and the full breadth of his shoulders were fully displayed.

I pinched my lips between my teeth to keep from groaning.

Forget the quilt, he was the coziest thing in this place.

Stop it. You do not lust after this man.

But I did.

I really did.

Chapter Fourteen

Alicia

I t was almost painful to admit, "You know, I want to be annoyed that the only snacks you had was cheddar cheese, apples, and peanut butter, but I'm really happy with this right now."

"Are you sure? You gave me a lot of shit just a few minutes ago." He shoved a peanut butter slathered slice of apple in his mouth.

"How do you not have a single potato chip in this place?"

He leveled narrowed eyes at me. "Because I ate them all. What do you do with *your* chips?"

"You're not being very considerate of your guests."

"You noticed all of those," he retorted sarcasm dripped from every word.

I lifted an eyebrow at the plate on the coffee table between us. "There was that woman at the clinic before my appointment a couple weeks ago."

Groaning, he pressed the back of his head into the headrest of his recliner. "Don't remind me."

We'd moved into the living room after he'd plated the snacks. The quilt was draped over my lap, and it was even better than I'd remembered—a warm, comforting weight as if there was more than fabric and thread holding it together. Furgie was curled up on the sofa next to me, watching his cat perched on a window shelf on the other side of the room. She'd only whined when he'd hissed at her, but we kept her leash on her lying on the cushion next to me.

After Remi had ensured that I was settled, he'd turned his attention to the fire in the stove.

"So, what happened there?" I sounded like the answer didn't matter to me, but if I was being fully honest with myself, it did matter. I didn't want him spending the rest of his life pining over me or anything, I would just like to not be unimportant to him. There were invisible marks all over me, divots in the essence of who I was because of him. I just wanted to be there on him too.

"Nothing."

"Okay, don't tell me. It'd probably be weird to have that conversation, anyway."

"No, really. Nothing happened there, and if you knew Lily her reaction wouldn't be that surprising to you."

"I could never put myself out there like that," I said. The temperature in the room dropped a few degrees. Of course we were thinking of the same thing.

There was one time I'd put myself out there. A single moment where my pride came second to my love for him.

A door closed in my face, leaving me out in the rain and wind.

He opened his mouth to speak, and panic cut hot and sharp through my nervous system—I didn't know what he planned to say but I wasn't ready for it. Instead, I asked, "What the hell was up with your scrubs that week?"

He barked a laugh. Just like that we fell back into the easy place we'd been a moment before.

Too excited for whatever story he was about to tell, I shifted to lean toward him.

"Nora." Shaking his head, he went on, "A couple of weeks ago, she challenged me to a push-up competition—"

"And she won?!"

"She did. She didn't wipe the floor with me or anything. I would like to say that I've dealt with my toxic masculinity, that I'm enough of a feminist for my pride to not take a hit. But it did. I was drunk, obviously."

"Obviously."

"Anyway, she's a beast and incredibly competitive. So, I got on my hands on the sticky dance floor of Benji's Place—"

"That's *the* bar in town, right?"

"Oh, yeah, there was a decent crowd of onlookers."

"What you're saying is if I needed protecting, I'd really want Nora to break through my door."

He splayed his hands out in front of himself. "Hold on, now."

"So, because she beat you, she got to pick your scrubs for a week?"

His nodding transformed into the shake of his head. "Yes."

"That's rough. But Lily still wanted you after that."

"Who'd a thunk it?"

I snorted. The smile on his face pressed creases into the corners of his twinkling eyes. A dusting of stubble made him appear both ruggedly handsome and a little vulnerable. Navy sweatpants draped across his long thighs.

I ignored the little voice in my head whispering, *I'd've thunk it.*

If it weren't for our history, I'd have a hard time not falling in love with him.

For a moment, the only sound was Furgie's gentle snores and the crackle of fire. Something passed in the air between us. A crackle. A sizzle. A spark. And suddenly, I couldn't look directly at him anymore.

Maybe I was more tired than I'd thought, it was the only explanation, because I would never . . . I'd learned my lesson; he'd taught it to me. I didn't yearn for a man the way I used to for him, and there was no way I'd ever go back there.

He cleared his throat. "Wanna watch something?"

"Yeahforsurethat'dbeawesome." My words jumbled together in their haste to get out of my mouth, anything to appear unaffected.

"What are you into these days?"

"Are you watching Sovereign?"

He scoffed. "Am I watching Sovereign?"

"There's a new season out."

"Oh, I know."

"Let me guess, you've watched like four or five episodes, and you're savoring it, and really taking time to think through all of the hints."

"You know me."

I do *know you*.

"God, I hated that. I just wanted to rot on the sofa and watch all ten episodes until three a.m."

"I'm gonna say you haven't even started it, yet, because you're focused on your work and it's this little prize you get to give yourself when you're done with this project."

"It is more than a little prize; it is a *big* one. I take this show very seriously."

"So, you *don't* want to watch it tonight?"

I pressed my fingertips to my lips, staring at the black television screen. "I kinda really want to watch it," I muttered into my fingers.

"Okay, fair warning." His chair creaked as he leaned forward, his forearms resting on his thighs. "The first episode ended on such a cliffhanger, I watched the second episode that same night."

"Oh shit," I breathed.

"Yeah."

"Turn it on."

"Are you sure?"

"Do not make me repeat myself."

He laughed. The sound warmed me from the inside.

The first episode we watched was packed with so much weird ass plot, that I forgot where I was. I audibly gasped at the end and turned to find Remi watching me with a lopsided grin.

"What *is* happening?" I demanded.

"Ready for bed?" He snorted at my unimpressed expression. "Next episode, then."

By the time we turned the television off, I was almost on the same episode he'd left off on, and the fire was red embers and black ash. I took Furgie out to go to the bathroom while he got his bed ready for me.

Rubbing my eyes, I yawned a goodnight on my way up the stairs to his room.

The sheets were clean, the fit snug and cozy the way only clean sheets could. He was on the sofa, but he was also still here, lingering deep in the fibers of his pillow. Just past the clean scent of his detergent was *him*—that smell I would know anywhere. That I'd never forget. That sat heavy and hot in my core. It pulled and tugged at me, urging me, reminding me.

As if his insinuated presence wasn't enough, flashes of him lit behind my eyelids. His sweatshirt sleeves pushed up as he shoveled my driveway in the morning sun. Steam burning off the skin stretched over his corded forearms. The fabric on his back clinging to his muscles flexing with each scrape and fling of snow. The memory of my hands on his bare skin as he moved over me.

I tried to change the channel in my mind but found a different memory instead. The moment when he burst into my apartment wild, raw, and dangerous. Midnight eyes searching over me, assessing. His switch to easy smiles and conversation—to *knowing* me as if time between us hadn't passed at all.

I shifted my hips, the ache between my thighs too uncomfortable to ignore.

I will not get off in my ex's bed.

I didn't.

But I also didn't sleep well all night.

Chapter Fifteen

Remi

"He might be groggy for a while, and his stomach might be sensitive for the rest of the day. I would keep him to a mild diet," I explained leading Ol' Man Terrance out of the exam room. I held his little dog, Sheriff, under one arm, his eyes were glassy, but he had come out of anesthesia nicely. Terrance hobbled along beside me with a cane gripped in his right hand. He'd slipped on some ice, and the healing was going slower than he'd like.

"Did you hear that, Sheriff? No sharin' my fuckin' ice cream tonight," Terrance said in his usual fuck-ridden dialect.

"It wouldn't make any difference if I told you dogs are lactose intolerant, would it?"

He harrumphed. "It makes him fuckin' happy. Let the dog fuckin' live."

"Fair enough." I accepted Terrance's keys in order to deliver his dog to the passenger seat while he paid the bill. When I got back inside, Terrance was almost to the vestibule.

Just inside, I held open the lobby door. "Thank you, again for being so understanding about the damage to my neighbor's apartment."

He owned the duplex that Alicia and I lived in, so it was really his property that I'd demolished.

"No fuckin' worries, son. You got that little flyin' fucker out of my house, and you're fixin' the fuckin' problem you made," he responded.

"I still appreciate it."

He paused just before the vestibule to face me. "That new neighbor of yours, she got a good car for this fuckin' snow?"

"Uh," I considered the nondescript SUV she drove. "I think so."

"Give her a fuckin' hand if she needs it. She works for some goddamn environmental firm in Chicago. I don't know if she's got the balls to make the fuckin' cut up here."

"I think she's good." I didn't point out that Chicago's winters were no joke. I also didn't tell him she'd grown up in a town just outside of Mackinaw City, that she knew exactly what to expect from February on the coast of Lake Michigan. It'd just spark more questions. So far, the town hadn't discovered that Alicia and I had been married. Once it did, it was going to run through every social group like wildfire. There was nothing that united this place like juicy gossip.

"You keep a fuckin' eye out for her, anyway. I hear she's a fuckin' looker, maybe you'll like the sight."

"Uh," was all I could manage for a moment. "Sure."

We waved goodbye. I chuckled as his voice carried from the outdoors through vestibule. "Shit on a goddamn dick it's fuckin' cold."

Nora snorted behind the front desk. Hazel was so focused on the chart opened next to her that she didn't seem to hear him. Her car was packed to leave directly from the office to visit her boyfriend, Elijah, in Detroit, so she was working as fast as possible to get on the road.

I shrugged. "At least the waiting room is empty with the mouth on that guy."

"Oh, I only schedule him when no one else will be here. I remember one time when I was a teenager, he swore in front of Lily and her mom lost her shit." She talked to her computer screen while typing. I didn't know how she could do it; I would have been typing everything I was saying. "And Ol' Terrance was just standing there with his arms out going, 'What'd I fuckin' say?' Some of the funniest shit I've ever seen."

Hazel snorted down at her chart.

My phone buzzed in my scrubs' pocket, and I paused halfway through the lobby reading Alicia's name on my screen. We'd exchanged numbers to coordinate my fixing her door, but still her presence on my phone sent a jolt through me. An excited bolt of lightning. Hanging out with her last night had been one of the most fun nights that I'd had in a while, even if we'd only chilled in my living room.

Sure, the whole time I had to fight the desire to be on the sofa with her, or the fantasy of her climbing onto my lap. Straddling me. My hands roaming over the curves of her body. My lips on her neck. My cock—

Yup, the problem had continued into today.

> Alicia: Is my door still held together by duct tape?

Me: Yeah, sorry, I have to ask Brooks if he can help me. It's been a crazy day. He's finishing his final appointment now.

> Alicia: Mission Unfuck my Door is still in motion.

Me: Can't put the genie back in the bottle.

> Alicia: Is that what you're calling it these days?

Me: Give it a rub and find out—

"Nope," I said out loud erasing the text before I could hit send.

> Alicia: Sorry, that was inappropriate or something.

> Alicia: Anyway, it's no big deal that it's not done, yet. I'm working late tonight.

> Alicia: I'd say let yourself in, but you really don't need encouragement.

> Me: *eyeroll emoji* You break down one door.

> Alicia: *GIF of Kool-Aid Man running through a wall* I'm only sending you this because, unfortunately, there isn't a gif of someone humping a door. Which seems unrealistic.

> Me: I'm not mad, Internet, I'm just disappoint-ed.

It was the quiet that I noticed first. Nora's typing had stopped, and I had the unnerving feeling of being watched. I looked up to find my coworkers staring at me. "What?"

They exchanged a silent conversation, a raised eyebrow from Hazel and a smirk from Nora. It didn't sit well. I slid my phone back where it was, as if that would hide away whatever they were reading into.

"Who're you texting?" Nora asked, a gleam in her eyes.

"It's nothing, I just need to do some work on my neighbor's place and we're coordinating." It was true, although not the whole truth, and even I found it suspicious that I chose to minimize the details.

"Your neighbor?" Hazel asked, at the same time Nora said, "Your ex-wife?"

Hazel's eyes widened. "Alicia's your *neighbor*?!"

I opened my mouth, but Nora spoke before me. "You didn't know?"

"*You* did?"

"Brooks told me."

Hazel glowered at me. "Apparently, I'm the last to find out you're co-habiting with your ex—"

I rolled my eyes. "We don't *live* together."

"You might as well! That wall is so thin." She crossed her arms over her chest and leaned back in her chair. "Why did you tell him and not me?"

I opened my mouth to explain, but Nora spoke first. "Is it that big of a deal?"

"You weren't there," Hazel exclaimed, and I struggled between compassion for my friend who was clearly feeling protective and irritation that she was making a big deal of everything. "She treated him like shit—"

"I wasn't exactly innocent," I pointed out, not that Hazel paid any attention.

"And when she finally served him divorce papers, out. Of. Nowhere—"

"There were warnings if I'd been willing to see them."

"He barely passed our senior finals and then fled the state."

"You make it sound like I was a fugitive."

"No, you just couldn't continue living your life. You had to run to the other side of the country, and fuck and drink your way through the state of Arizona." A flash of uncertainty lit across Hazel's features; I could practically hear her wondering if she'd gone too far.

I didn't know if she had either.

Suddenly the vaguely flirty texts didn't seem as fun as they had been just a moment ago.

I swallowed with my jaw set.

Nora's gaze flicked between me and Hazel.

"It's not . . ." I began, searching for the right words. "It's not like that . . . anymore."

Hazel fidgeted with a crease in the pant leg of her scrubs. "What's different?"

"Me," I said simply. "Her."

She lifted an eyebrow.

"You never got to see the best in her, because you were only seeing her through me, and she wasn't getting my best either." I rubbed my palm along my jaw, wrestling with what to say next.

"We're different," I went on. "We're just two people who used to know each other, and for a little while we'll occupy space nearby each other."

Hazel gripped the end of her braid. "Just . . . be careful."

"I don't have to be, because there's nothing there anymore," I lied.

It didn't matter that to this day, Alicia still burned inside every molecule of my body; I was one everlasting flame. I *knew* her. She'd never let her guard down with me like that again. Not after that night in the rain.

It didn't matter that I carried a flame I couldn't put out. Or that it grew stronger with each interaction, text, glance. My feelings for Alicia were more like catching the essence of something out of the corner of my eye, something I wasn't capable of dissecting. I just couldn't fully deny it—not when I ran through a door, not when her every laugh made me smile or the fact that my little apartment hadn't felt like home until she was in it.

I could package my emotions into neat little boxes and tell myself that I just wanted to make things right or find closure. It wasn't a lie. It just wasn't the whole truth.

I wanted Alicia in any way that I could have her, even if for just a short while.

"You don't have to worry," I said, sounding cheerier than I felt. "She'll do her job and go back to Chicago. There's nothing to worry about. Also, it looks like I'm off the hook with Lily."

"Oh, shit, yeah, she's got that new guy from Darling," Nora said the last word like it tasted disgusting. I didn't quite understand the Grand Ridge hatred of the neighboring town of Darling, but nothing made them more angry than its existence.

"Get drinks to celebrate tonight?"

"Not like there's anything else to do." She went back to her typing.

Hazel's shoulders relaxed away from her ears. She wasn't fully satisfied, but she wouldn't push it further.

Chapter Sixteen

Remi

B rooks' thick, dark brows drew together, and his bright blue eyes
flicked from corner to corner of Alicia's demolished door frame.
It looked worse under the bright clamp light he'd set up—it was early
evening, and the sun had already set. Wood had splintered and the door
frame was only half there. The door itself had a hole roughly the size of
my shoulder covered in duct-tape and cardboard. Long, sharp shadows
drew across it like the teeth of an open mouth.

After a few seconds, he asked, "What happened?"

I cleared my throat. "There was a bird."

"A bird did this?" he exclaimed in a rare expression of emotion, his
eyes wide with shock.

"No." I coughed a chuckle. "I did."

He blinked, and I wanted to explain, but his stare was a bit like being
under a microscope.

Scratching my eyebrow, I shrugged. "She screamed."

The fear that had gripped me when I'd heard it flashed brightly in my
mind, the cold determination to do whatever it took to keep her safe.
Not my neighbor. Not just any other person. But to keep *her* safe.

"And you knocked really hard?" he deadpanned.

Some of the pressure in my chest loosened. "Fuck you, man. Can you
help me fix it?"

"Do you have the door and frame?"

"Yeah." I gestured toward my carport where everything leaned against the duplex just out of sight.

"We can get this done." He set his toolbox on the porch and bent to look inside of it. "So, there was a bird?"

"A good-sized bird." I smiled a bit at using her words from last night; they sounded as feeble from me as they had from her.

Standing, he held a crowbar in one hand and took a step toward the door and began prying the pieces apart. "She screamed because of the bird, and you ran *through* the door."

I rocked my weight from my toes to my heels. "I didn't know what she was screaming about."

For a moment, the only sound was the screech of metal nails pulled free from wood. In the lack of conversation, my nerves rattled around inside of my head, and I couldn't just keep quiet. I needed to *try* to justify my reaction. Overreaction, really.

"The dog was barking too," I said.

"So outta character for a dog," he acknowledged with the driest tone. "Nah, it's okay. I get it."

"Get what?" Heat began to climb up my neck despite the dropping temperature.

He cut a look my way, and that was all he needed to do to express a very clear, *Don't bullshit me.* The man was practically a bloodhound for anyone else's bullshit. And whatever he'd seen in the front I had up, he recognized—turning me to face the truth. The reality I continued to struggle with but was taking too clear a form to struggle any longer.

"How'd she handle all of this?" he asked.

"Fine. Initially, she was annoyed that I wanted her to stay at my place until her door could get fixed, but that was it."

He stilled, before turning to face me. "She spent the night with you?"

"Not like that." I ignored the way even the implication of sharing a bed with her made my blood heat. "I was on the couch. We just watched a show and hung out a bit."

He made a, *huh*, sound, then went back to work on the door.

I scratched where the collar of my coat rubbed against my neck. "What?"

"I'd get a hotel room before I stayed with any of my ex's."

"There was no reason, we made it work."

"I thought it was a bad break up."

"It was. Really bad."

He did that infuriating, *huh*, sound again.

"What?" The word came out sharper this second time around.

"Just . . . a little while ago you almost fell off of Stone because she walked in the arena, and now you're watching shows and hanging out. Not a trajectory I would expect. It's just kinda confusing."

"Weren't you the one that suggested I could make things right with her?"

"Yeah, but I didn't think it'd look like you two becoming"—he flicked his eyes toward me, placing me, once again, under the microscope—"*friends*."

"I ran through her door, and it wasn't safe for her to stay here. I don't know if I'd call us friends."

Denying the connection between us felt unnatural. The more I did, the less convincing it felt—like saying, *Don't think about an elephant.* But then for me the saying was, *Don't think about how you've harbored an empty, aching need inside of your chest since you left Alicia alone in the rain*, and then it was all I could think about. And worse, it made me realize that the pain lessened when she was near. But I'd already ruined everything.

I didn't deserve what my feelings were shaping into.

Fulfilling this gnawing want was out of reach, I'd already blown up my chances with her years ago. Not only had I abolished our relationship one shitty comment or passive aggressive action after the other, I'd taken her most vulnerable moment and I'd shoved it in her face. I'd been too angry, and lonely, and unwilling to accept my responsibility for my life to accept the rail thin peace offering she'd begged me to take. The apartment I'd moved into after we split up was empty and depressing. Her hands clutched the signed divorce papers. Rain dripped from the ends of her hair, mixing with the tears on her cheeks and chin.

"I'll tear them up," she offered, shaking the damp contracts. "I'll go to counseling with you. I'll . . . I don't even know. I don't know what to do. But I will never love anyone like I love you. I don't even want to. Never. Only you. Please, tell me you'll do whatever it takes, and I will too."

Her shoulders shook and her words were swallowed in her sobs.

I should have held her. Kissed her.

Apologized.

Promised.

"I don't want to live this life without you," she forced out. It was almost impossible to understand her, but the words rang true inside of my chest. But they just made me angry.

And scared.

I couldn't even identify what I was afraid of, but I wanted to run away.

So, I didn't speak. I didn't do any of the things that I should have done.

I just closed the door.

I'd ruined my chances with the woman I didn't want to live this life without.

"That door is closed," I muttered more to myself than to him.

He grunted. Turning back to the repair, he said, "Closed doors don't seem to stop you."

Chapter Seventeen

Remi

B enji's Place was packed. Clearly, the entire town had come out to drink and spend time with their neighbors, breaking free from the shut-in feeling of winter. Temporary igloos were set up on the patio, and we'd been lucky to snag one. I'd arrived at the bar after Brooks and I fixed Alicia's door. He had something to do at Nora's grandma's house before joining me.

I had just parked my car when Sterling and his sister, Bet, flagged me down. The sun had set about an hour before—even though it was only mid-evening, it looked like the middle of the night. It was early enough that Bet's two-year-old, Melody, was falling asleep on my chest, while her four-year-old, Sasha, laughed at a game she was playing with her Uncle Sterling.

I wanted to settle into my usual Saturday routine, but I couldn't stop checking my phone for a reply from Alicia. I'd sent, *Your apartment is a bird-free fortress*, about two hours ago, and I needed to stop fixating as I scanned for her car in the parking lot, even though all I could see were headlights piercing the night before they blotted out leaving behind a blind spot in my vision. She hadn't said that she'd be here. We weren't planning to meet up. There wasn't any excuse to text anymore, but I knew she was somewhere near, making it impossible to relax.

Bet stared up at the inky sky, her hot chocolate steaming in her mug.

"A cow does not say, 'bark!' " Sterling exclaimed.

Sasha giggled around her fingers.

He narrowed his eyes at her, but like everyone else, she didn't take him seriously. "What *does* a cow say?"

She narrowed her eyes back, a smile growing on her face. "Quack."

It was the quack that broke his serious facade, and the rest of us joined in the laughter. Not Melody, though.

"She is out." Bet's bright blue eyes were soft and adoring on her daughter's face. All the Strauss siblings had the same startling-colored eyes, except for the youngest, Violet.

"If this chair was more comfortable, I'd be sleeping too," I said.

"Thank you, by the way. I needed a break." She exhaled closing her eyes. "But I should get them home and to bed."

A gust of cold air swept into the igloo as Lola, Bet and Sterling's other sister, joined us.

"I'll carry Mel out to your car," I offered.

Lola leaned against Bet's chair. Her large curls were pulled back into a ponytail high on her head, and her olive-green sweater clung to her curves. She winked at me, and I smirked back. We'd dated briefly but quickly decided that we were better as friends. In weak moments, I wondered if it was a shortcoming on my end that we couldn't be more. She was great. Smart. Beautiful. Fun.

But there was the ever-lingering afterimage of Alicia etched into the future I imagined. Taking up too much space for anyone else to fit.

"Are you leaving already?" Lola asked.

Bet sighed. "I should, but I don't think I can. I'm not ready."

Lola tilted her head, grinning at her niece's sleeping face. "I kinda wanna steal her from you."

"Take a seat." I jerked my head toward a vacant spot at our table.

"I wouldn't want to wake her up."

"You're missing out."

"I know," she sighed.

Sterling scoffed. "Kiss already."

Lola blushed and rolled her eyes, and for a moment there was a perfect snapshot of what it was like for her to grow up with Sterling as a younger, louder brother.

"That's what you want to see?" I asked.

Faking a gag, Bet said, "You know what, maybe I am ready to leave."

"You're not into that?" Lola mocked. "Watching your sister kiss someone? How very normal of you."

"In Sterling's defense, no one has ever accused him of being normal."

Without looking away from Sasha, Sterling retorted, "You wouldn't take me any other way."

Bet leaned past Lola. "Are you giving me an option?"

Lola's eyebrows climbed up her forehead. "I'd love to go a week without hearing *something* about you."

"It's not that bad." He rocked back and forth with Sasha holding his thumbs giggling.

"I will not have you telling me what is or is not bad with the things I have heard . . ."

Slowly shaking her head, Bet grimaced. "More than any sister would ever want to know."

"You should make them sign an NDA. It'd be a public service." Lola lifted her drink to her lips.

With a shit-eating grin, Sterling said, "I like to think of it that way too."

Both of his sister's faces twisted in disgust.

I muffled my laugh, careful not to jostle Melody.

"Speaking of things people say," Sterling began. "Remi, your name has been thrown around quite a bit lately."

A sharp spike of unease needled just under my ribcage. "Yeah?"

"Leave him alone," Bet scolded.

"You're not curious?"

"Ignore him," Lola told me.

"About what?" I knew what he was talking about, and I would rather have this conversation with them instead of some other people in town. The news could travel from their lips; mine and Alicia's past was bound to come out eventually.

Sterling narrowed his eyes at me. "First, Lily—"

"First nothing, you know that's bull"—I cut myself off, glancing at Sasha's sweet face—"hockery."

"Nice save," Bet laughed.

"Thank you."

"All right but then explain this new neighbor."

"Alicia?"

"Is she really your ex-wife?"

"Yeah, Alicia and I were married." I answered as if it was no big deal. It *was* a matter of fact. Nothing scandalous. People got married and divorced for all sorts of reasons. The only reason it was notable was because we were in the same small town and sharing a duplex as luck would have it. The news might have been new to them, but I'd processed through it. The resurfacing of old feelings—ones that had never really settled—remained in process. Since my reaction to hearing one scream from her, and the conversation at the office earlier, followed by Brooks kinda sorta calling me out, the truth of the situation had grown into something more clear and obvious.

I'd expected . . . something other than the awkward silence where no one would look at me, as if they already knew what I'd only just realized.

It probably only lasted two or three seconds, but it felt longer. Racking my brain for a natural change of subject, I lifted my beer and swallowed the malty fizzing liquid.

Finally, Bet said, "The girls and I met her at the library. She asked me to sign her petition for the wetlands."

I nodded. "Yeah, she's doing good work."

"She seems cool."

"She is."

Sterling scrunched his nose at his niece. "I ran into her at the café a few weeks ago. She's *really* pretty."

It wasn't that I didn't like him noticing. Alicia was more than pretty. She was a knockout—a goddamn fox. She was the most exquisitely beautiful woman to ever grace this earth. Looking at her was like looking at a sunset, vibrant and full of color. She could stop my heart with just her eyes meeting mine, and make it race with the curve of her lips. And that said nothing about the perfect unworldly experience of seeing her naked.

I just didn't like *him* noticing. I didn't think he'd ever been rejected by anyone. Ever.

Meanwhile, I'd already rejected Alicia.

What a fool.

Mustering a nonchalance I did not feel, I said, "I've always thought so."

Sasha placed her tiny hands on both sides of Sterling's face and urged him to look at her.

He kissed her forehead. "Sorry, goofball, was I not paying enough attention to you?"

Her little eyebrow furrowed and she grunted.

"She's getting grumpy," Bet muttered.

With her voice lowered to speak only to me, Lola asked, "Are you okay?"

"Why wouldn't I be okay?"

She tilted her head. "I just wanted to check."

"I'm good, Lo." I hoped she believed me.

"I think if my ex moved in next door, I might not be quite right about it."

"It was weird, at first. I'm past it now."

"Good."

But my phone continued to not receive a response from Alicia, and I was still searching for her headlights breaking through the night. The knowledge that I was completely full of shit had grown past the point of ignoring. My need to be near her was bad for my health, and persistent. My feelings were more than residual. And she was more than a representation of my past wrong doings that I wanted to make right.

I was still in love with Alicia.

Chapter Eighteen

Alicia

T hrough my windshield played the sweetest little tableau. A sleeping baby hugged to Remi's chest. A gorgeous brunette walking next to him. They were talking as if this was the most normal thing in the world. She put an older little girl in her seat, before rounding the trunk of her car to check the straps of the car seat Remi had deposited the youngest in. Even from this distance with only the parking lot lights overhead, I could tell her eyes were the clearest blue, that her cheekbones were high, and under her wide lips was a delicate, pointed chin.

In short, she was absolutely lovely.

But when they hugged goodbye it didn't linger. Not that it mattered.

It didn't matter.

It just made it feel like snakes were slithering in my stomach.

I erased the text I'd been typing just a moment before thanking him for fixing the door he broke. I'd gone back and forth on replying but ultimately decided I would for two reasons. One, it'd been fun to talk to him throughout the day. And two, I really wanted to bury that text I'd sent about him calling his penis a genie.

So embarrassing.

It was even worse that he didn't even acknowledge that I said it.

"What response could he have made to make that comment okay?" I spoke aloud to my empty car.

Remi waved goodbye to the gorgeous mom.

Admitting, even to myself, that I felt the slightest twinge of envy over who Remi spent time with was humiliating.

I couldn't even bring myself to tell Sadie that I was getting tied up in a weird almost friendship with him. Her advice and perspective would be helpful, but then I'd have to admit that I was less than indifferent toward him. And she'd be able to tell that I was lying when I said these feelings had nothing to do with attraction not only to his appearance but . . . *him*.

Remaining in my car, as he jogged back to the building. I sent a simple, *Thanks*.

He slowed to a halt, pulling his phone out of his back pocket. The steam of his breath shone in the parking lot light; it illuminated him in stark contrasts. His thumbs hovered above the screen of his phone before tapping haltingly. Furrows dug deep into his forehead. One giant puff of silver blotted against the black sky and then disappeared. His shoulders fell, his face pointed up.

My heart twisted.

This one-sided unguarded display.

This confirmation that our situation wasn't easy on him either.

He slid his phone back into his pocket. With less spring in his step than before, he took long strides toward the building.

The ache in my chest moved upward squeezing like a fist around my throat.

"What are we doing?" I whispered.

Nothing, I pointed out. *Absolutely nothing, we are existing. We are withstanding a shitty situation. And we're doing a pretty good goddamn job of it.*

Anyway, I was here with Emmett—in a professional capacity only, but still. He had offered to introduce me to people who would be able to spread the news about my cause. I'd established a rule years ago that while

I was traveling for work: I did not pursue anyone romantically. Part of my job, possibly the most important aspect, was being likable. Entering into a small dating scene . . . It wasn't good for business. I needed all the help I could get. Gaining traction within Grand Ridge had been slower than I'd expected. If everything didn't sound promising for Jamison, lawyer fuckboy, at the capitol then I would be nervous about my progress.

Plus, Emmett seemed really nice. I had every reason to enjoy his company—and zero reasons to be jealous of the company my ex-husband kept.

Still, I found myself both dreading and anticipating getting to snag glances of Remi in the wild, among the people he filled his time with. Dread won out when I considered that he might do more than hug someone tonight.

"Get your head outta your ass," I demanded, truly fed-up with my bullshit.

I took a bracing breath and stepped out of my car.

Entering the building, I was grateful that I'd left my bulky coat on my passenger seat. The place was packed and warm. I had to weave around groups, perfumes and body odor mixed with the smell of alcohol. But I'd only found one sticky spot on the floor from a spilled beverage, so the patrons weren't too rowdy, yet.

Emmett was where he had promised to be. He leaned one elbow on the bar sipping his beer. Missy sat on a stool next to him.

Her blond hair was pulled into a simple bun, combined with her oversized, black-rimmed glasses and loose-fitting black tunic she looked far too sophisticated for the area, let alone the bar—which was nice in a rugged kind of way. The walls were lined with wooden booths. Circular tables stood in the center, and black steel beams stretched across the ceiling. A large well-lit mirror hung behind tiers of alcohol.

When Emmett spotted me, he straightened and a little smile pulled at his lips.

He was slightly taller than the average man, and the trim fit of his blue sweater and jeans elongated his frame. His strong jaw was covered in a full, black beard, and his dark brown eyes were lined in long swooping lashes.

"You made it," Missy said, her voice deep for such a tiny woman.

Lifting his beer off the bar, Emmett offered, "Do you want a drink?"

I couldn't keep myself from scanning the packed room. If Remi was in it, I'd spot him. Not just because he was taller than most of the human race, but because my eyes liked to find him. They would land on him no matter where we found ourselves.

Not for the first time, I reminded myself, *Noticing is not the same as action.*

Had I taken an eyeful of my ex-husband that morning? The sprawl of his frame on the sofa, too big to fit. The fine lines from the corners of his eyes. His slightly parted perfectly shaped pink lips. The reddish brown of his eyelashes and in the stubble on his jaw warm against his skin.

Yes.

Had it rekindled the desire I'd struggled with all night?

Again, yes.

Had I acted on my unfortunately lusty thoughts?

No.

I'd learned the hard way to be mindful of my choices.

"Yeah, do they have a wine list?" I asked.

Missy pinched a laminated white piece of paper between her fingers and handed it to me.

Emmett leaned against the bar on his elbow. "How's the petition coming?"

"I'm making progress." I left out the fact that it was coming too slowly.

"You'll get to meet pretty much everyone tonight." Missy lifted her cocktail and scanned the crowd. "Bet Strauss just left, but Lola or Sterling might still be here. Just a warning, Sterling is the worst flirt."

A muscle flexed in Emmett's jaw.

I recalled the charming man with dark hair and blue eyes at the coffee shop on my first day in town. "I think I met him already."

"He'd be good to get on your team," Emmett said. "So would Hazel from the animal hospital, but I haven't seen her."

"I know her, actually." My cheeks flushed, unexpectedly. "She was Remi's classmate, when he and I were married."

"Married?" Missy's thin eyebrows arched.

"Yeah, but it was a long time ago," I explained, even though it wasn't really their business.

Emmett had frozen with his beer halfway to his lips. "What are the odds of that?"

Missy's face had gone blank. It was seamless, as if she'd practiced for her therapy sessions. "Have you kept in touch since the divorce?"

I huffed a laugh. "No."

"So, this came as a shock?"

"Oh, yes."

"Well, I hope this reconnection is positive."

"It's been weird." I paused, considering. "But I'd say positive."

"That's wonderful." She smiled, and I wondered what she was thinking behind her gray eyes.

"It is," I agreed.

"Anyway, you should meet Benji." She held up a delicate finger and called in a voice that somehow carried over the laughter and talking around us without being loud, "Ben."

A few feet away a man with the sandy brown hair poured a beer from behind the bar. "You done with your Manhattan already, Miss?"

"No, come over here."

He looked in our direction, then did that very flattering thing, where his eyes snagged on me before widening.

Missy rubbed below her ear. "Heads up, he's a bit of a flirt too."

Benji took a few steps toward us wiping his hands on the towel over his shoulder. "Hi I'm Ben."

"*The* Ben of Benji's Place?"

His eyes got extra crinkly as his smile broadened. "That's me. And you're Alicia."

"How did you know?"

He tilted his head toward Emmett. "Deb called me a couple of days ago and said you're here with a mission."

"Your mom is a gem," I told Emmett.

"She's great. She's my aunt actually." Ben circled his finger indicating Missy and Emmett. "We all grew up together."

"Are you their cousin too?" I asked Missy.

She shook her head emphatically. "No. Family friends."

"I wanna to talk to you, but I'm on my way out. Can I get your number to set up a meeting? See how I can help out?"

"Yes, please." I would take all the help I could get.

He snagged an order pad and I jotted my information down. Promising to set something up with me, he waved goodbye.

Missy left shortly after finishing her cocktail, claiming that Ben made the best Manhattans. Emmett watched her leave, and the briefest flash of longing surfaced in the depths of his eyes. I wondered if she knew. If she understood it. The unfulfilled need that surpassed desire. The way it could bore into your soul and make you want the one thing you couldn't have—something so far out of reach you couldn't even voice it to your closest friend.

I slipped onto her vacated barstool, pretending like I didn't notice anything, as if I didn't feel gutted by proxy.

We fell into an easy conversation about our work, and as people passed by he'd call them over for an introduction. Somehow I'd drank a glass and half of white wine from some local winery when the backdoor to the patio swung open, carrying new voices and laughter over the din of the bar. The receptionist from Remi's vet clinic walked side-by-side with a shaggy haired man I vaguely recognized.

Then there was Remi.

My stomach dropped like falling down the first hill of a roller coaster. The lights brightened, and I swear I could hear them buzzing over everything else. A shiver ran down my spine that I tried to hide by taking a drink of my Chardonnay.

But *I* knew it was there.

Chapter Nineteen

Alicia

E mmett was a great distraction. He had a mellow energy, but he seemed genuinely interested our conversation about nature conservation. It was a great talk. So much so, that I barely noticed when Remi joined some of his friends on the dance floor. I was too preoccupied by Emmett's thoughtful observations to give Remi's huge smile as he swayed from side-to-side any of my attention. Emmett sharing the names of influential people in the county held my complete consciousness. So preoccupying that I didn't pay any attention to the flex of Remi's thighs in his jeans—it was obscene.

I was ignoring his existence so effectively that when Emmett excused himself for a few moments, I was able to feign surprise as Remi leaned his elbows on the bar a few stools down from where I sat. The friendly smile he gave me was just like the one from that morning after checking that my side of the wall was safe enough for me to enter.

We were friendly, and wasn't that good? Wasn't that great? It actually wasn't confusing or important at all. I didn't need to parcel out my impulse to talk to him or my desire to touch him.

Friends touched. I was sure of it. I was well practiced in having friends. One little touch.

My two glasses of Chardonnay agreed.

"You're everywhere these days," I called over the noise and music.

Remi's grin grew slowly, tying my heart strings into knots. "Not a whole lot of places to go."

"Having fun tonight?"

It was all the invitation he needed to move closer.

The crowd parted around him, giving way to his size. People here were a bit taller on average than most places, and yet, he was inches taller than everyone else. His chest was too large to squeeze between me and the person next to me. Instead, he gripped the edge of the bar with one hand, putting him partially beside and behind me. I always loved how he consumed space. The sheer mass of him surrounding me. Heat ebbed from his body, and under his clean scent was the bite of sweat.

I squirmed, all too aware of the ache between my thighs.

"I am," he answered. "You?"

"The wine is pretty good," I said lifting my glass to my lips, only to realize it was empty.

His eyes flicked from the glass to my face, I could practically see him holding back a comment.

"Don't," I warned, but there was no denying the humor in that single word.

"Wouldn't dream of it."

"Yes, you would."

God, that smile again, I groaned internally.

He had a jaw sharp enough to cut through my better judgment.

Not today, handsome man. But another much more muffled part of me whispered, *Well, maybe.*

Remi held up a hand to get the attention of the bartender. "Have you had their pretzels?"

"Oo! A pretzel!" I sat up straighter, instantly energized for some carbs.

"You're gonna love this one, the beer cheese will make you see God."

"You wanna"—I cut myself off from asking him if *he* could make me see God. It was like I'd lost all control over the horny little comments that should have stayed in my head and not *texted* to him or spoken—"share it with me?"

"Nah, I wouldn't want to crowd you and Emmett." The skin of his knuckles whitened as his grip tightened on bar.

I smirked down at my hands. *Don't be jealous, Remi, it's annoyingly hot.*

Okay, now he should go.

"We're just . . . there's nothing . . ." I chewed my lower lip, and heat rose up my cheeks as he glared down at the press of my teeth against my flesh. "He's just helping me."

"Save the wetlands?"

"All of them," I deadpanned.

"I believe in you." It could have been said in sarcasm, it would have worked just fine with our normal conversations. But it wasn't. Instead, there was sincerity in the timbre of his voice. It rumbled through my blood, coursing my waning confidence to grow. Affection burned in my chest, it felt good to be believed in.

"Thanks," I said lamely.

"So, why this state land?"

I opened my mouth prepared to tell him the tale I was telling everyone else before closing it again. Tilting my head to the side, I considered that I *knew* him. And that allowed a different kind of trust.

The nail of my thumb clicked on the bar top as I thought.

He lifted an eyebrow toward my nervous hand. "What are you thinking about?"

I leaned in, lowering my voice. "You wanna know the real reason?"

His midnight eyes sparkled. "Yes."

"You can't tell anyone. I shouldn't tell you."

"To the grave, Leese."

I couldn't help smiling. We both loved a secret. "The property was supposed to go to public auction, and we had a private benefactor prepared to buy and put protection covenants all over it."

"Good."

"But then they released the property list without this one on it, so I looked into it and saw a proposed development, and looked into the company, and found that a main investor is the son of a state congressman."

He mouthed *Oh*. "So, not only is it an abuse of natural resources, but an abuse of nepotism."

"Or as I like to call it, nepotism."

His laugh thundered down my skin—rich and messy. A storm I should seek shelter from, but it was too beautiful and wild to look away. I wanted to be swept up in it, soaked through. Get thrashed about, lost at sea, and whatever else this moment could give me.

One little touch.

The thermal cotton stretched across his chest was soft under my palm. And the muscle beneath was firm. His heartbeat drummed, and his breathing grew a bit strained—faster but measured. Did my sense of smell grow more acute? Or had he always smelled a little bit like . . . something smokey, I couldn't put my finger on it.

His crew neck rested on his collarbone. The tips of my fingers brushed a little higher, finding the skin just above the cotton. He was so hot . . . to the touch. It was as if I hadn't felt heat in years, and it was just there under the swirls of my fingerprints.

I flicked my gaze up to find his heavy-lidded eyes locked onto me. Looking at Remi was easy, my eyes slid from detail-to-detail, eating him up like a well-balanced diet.

But being seen by him, that made me squirm. He saw too much, laid me bare. Exposed.

I loved it.

Snatching my hand back, I lifted my glass to my lips only to remember that it was empty.

Still.

There was a possibility that I was more sloppy than I'd realized. It'd only been two glasses. Was I starving? Had I drank on an empty stomach? I hadn't felt this drunk before he'd come over, before he'd taken my space and breathed my air. A pressure, a pull, edging me off balance.

Blinking, he looked away. He lifted his beer to his lips and took a long drink, the muscles of his neck flexing.

"Hey," a perky voice said from the other side of the bar.

I startled, almost knocking over my glass.

"What can I get for you?" The tiny blond bartender flicked her eyes between us.

He pointed in my direction. "A pretzel with beer cheese, and"—he spoke to me—"and a water?"

To the woman behind the bar, I nodded. "A water would be great."

"No ice?" he asked.

The corners of my lips quirked upward—he remembered so many little things. "Yup, no ice, please."

He lifted his beer. "Two more of these, please."

"Sure thing."

A weird silence stretched between us as she walked away. I'd forgotten everything I'd ever learned about socializing. It was usually so easy for me to make conversation, but I kept stepping in patches that looked innocuous only to find a bees nest under my foot. I should have found myself covered in little stings, except I wasn't.

Liking Remi should hurt, right?

It shouldn't feel so easy to make him laugh or to be in his company. And yet, it was like the inhale and exhale of my breath—it didn't take any thought at all.

Even in this lack of anything to talk about, it was strange not because it was awkward but because it was comfortable.

The bartender set two longnecks on the bar in front of him and a water in front of me.

After thanking her, he turned to me. "If you and Emmett wanna join us there's room at our table."

"That's nice of you, but I'm actually here for work, so I'm gonna keep doing that." Jerking my head toward the glass in front of me, I went on. "I'll drink this and stop being a mess. I swear I haven't drank much, I think I forgot to eat today."

"I figured."

"Go back to having fun. Just pretend like I'm not even here," I said.

He scoffed but didn't say any more. He didn't need to.

The pink tip of his tongue flicked over his bottom lip leaving it wet and glistening. My breathing shallowed. I shifted on my barstool, crossing one leg over the other, a thrum of need unfurling low in my belly. He rubbed his long fingers on his mouth, wiping it dry. The memory of that touch burning along my skin made the hairs on my arms and the nape of my neck stand on end.

He jerked a nod and took a step back. The deep gruff set of his voice belied his polite words. "Have a good night, then, Leese."

"It's nice," I said quickly, making him pause in his retreat, "that we can be friends. I didn't think . . . I'm just glad we can be friends."

He exhaled one long breath before nodding. His back disappeared into the crowd, but the top of his head remained visible above everyone else's. I should look away, pretend like he wasn't even there, but I couldn't bring myself to. Until he turned and caught me staring.

My face burned and my pale-blue painted nails grew very interesting.

Emmett came back.

I forced a smile.

Chapter Twenty

Remi

I was not having fun anymore.

I wasn't even able to pretend that I was. Sitting alone in a booth pounding water was a vibe—I was technically good to drive, at this point it wasn't the alcohol affecting my judgment. The skin on my chest still tickled where Alicia's fingers had been. She was laughing and talking with Emmett and the people he introduced her to.

I was a full head of hare-brained ideas.

She needed to know, right? It wasn't fair for me to keep her in the dark that I couldn't be just her friend. It was unfair to let her believe I was capable of supporting her without the emotional turmoil and angst of wanting to repair our broken bond, of dreaming of a future where I could openly love her. I would have to tell her, eventually. Not tonight. There wasn't much different between my blissful ignorance of that morning when I still believed that our relationship could be casual—as casual as our sexual chemistry would allow—and where I found myself now. I'd come to my emotional realization, but other than that, everything was the same.

From my booth, I watched her wave goodbye, and I waited for relief to wash over me.

Instead, as she moved toward the door to leave I wrestled with the desire to follow her.

Give her space. Give yourself space.

It was good advice that I ignored. I launched out of my booth forcing myself to maneuver through the crowd at a reasonable pace and not move people out of my way. Just because I could didn't mean that I should. The route gave me time to put together what to say. There were three basic points: none of this was her fault, I would do a better job giving her distance, but I was still in love with her.

The last sentiment was a bit sticky. I was prepared to read the room, but I didn't know how I could tell her the other two points without the context of the last point.

Alicia was a few feet from her car with her keys in her hand, when I exited the building. Jogging, I closed the distance between us and called her name. She turned, her arms crossed under her breasts, pushing them up against the V-neck of her sweater and all my thoughts burned out of my mind. Sizzling into nothing as I came to a stop about five feet away from her. I shoved my hands in my pocket to keep from reaching out, she looked cold and soft and . . . boobs.

Fuck.

She shivered once, her brown eyes silently nudging me.

"Shit, sorry," I said but I wasn't sure what I was apologizing for.

"It's okay, what's up?" Her body shuddered again.

I gripped the bottom of my thermal shirt and tugged it free from my jeans before even considering my actions.

"What are you doing?" she demanded through chattering teeth.

"Giving you my shirt."

"No, don't"—she cut off as I pulled the clothes over my head.

Shaking my hair out of my eyes, I was more aware of the cold now that I was only in a thin, white T-shirt. I held the thermal toward her overly aware of her parted lips and her gaze moving from my chest, to my shoulders, to my biceps. With slow distracted movements, she took the garment from me and tugged it over her head.

She had to be freezing still. So, I needed to say what was necessary and put the needed distance between us. But finalizing my scattered thoughts into a cohesive statement, wasn't going well. Helpfully, when my shirt settled on her shoulders there might be an inch or two of her skin below her clavicle showing. Less distractions.

The top of her head broke through the neckline like fire burning through ash. The tips of her fingers curled over the ends of the shirt sleeves and hugged the fabric against her chest. She brought the collar to her nose and breathed in lowering her eyelids for the barest moment, casting a spell and stealing my breath.

We stood stock still.

I was lost in a slide show of the times she'd bewitched me.

The first moment I'd laid eyes on her as a freshman in undergrad. Pulling away from her after our first kiss with my heart pounding too loudly in my ears. Her chin high as she wore her white wedding gown, the distance between us closing step by step and I knew at the soul of my being I'd never stop loving her.

How right that young man had been.

"Remi?" she spoke, her voice a soft mist of steam.

"Yeah," I managed.

"What do you need?"

You.

I ran a hand down my face, letting it rest over my heart.

What did I need?

I had no idea, anymore.

Clearing my throat, I took a step back. "Uh . . ." Inside my mind, I scavenged through dusty corners to bring forward any thought that might be helpful in that moment. Because even though I'd followed after her hoping to gain distance, it was the last thing I wanted.

"Uh . . ." I said again before snapping my fingers when the idea came to me. "Your petition. I'll put a copy at the clinic; can't believe I didn't think to offer sooner."

The smile spread across her face looked a little relieved. "Thank you, that'd be a huge help."

"Sure." I cleared my throat. "I'll . . . see you around."

"I'm sure you will."

My boot scraped on the worn asphalt putting my back to her. I took quick steps back to the building, listening as she closed her drivers' side door behind her and drove away. Just outside the bar I changed my mind. Turning, I hurried to my vehicle. Behind the wheel I pushed the button to start it, dialing Owen's number simultaneously. The phone rang so many times that I almost gave up on him answering.

"Hey," he said in his usual relaxed way. In the background, Emmeline was having an argument with a number of other voices that I didn't recognize.

"Hey, man," I said, suddenly aware that I, once again, had no idea how to put everything into words. "You sound busy, I'll let you go."

"Nah, I'm good. Em's cousin, and brother, and brother in-law are here but they're good without me for a while. What's up?"

I'd met Owen in vet school, and he might have a bad response to all things Alicia just like Hazel did. I considered pretending like I just called to catch up but decided against it. He knew more about my feelings over the past couple of years, about how I regretted the way my marriage ended and the role I played in it. I hoped that was enough for him to keep a level head.

After a long pause, I admitted, "I'm messed up right now, man."

"What about?" he asked even though I was sure he could make an assumption.

"I need you to be cool about it."

He let out a long slow breath. "Alicia."

I grunted an affirmation.

"Okay." He sounded calm.

"I'm still in love with her." It felt strange to say it out loud, even if it was so obvious. "And I just followed her out of a bar to tell her to stay away from me, I think."

"You think?"

"I don't know exactly what I was going to say, but I chickened out. It was something like, 'I'm in love with you, and I'm gonna stay away from you, and you should stay away from me.' "

"Good thing you didn't."

"Is it?"

"Rem, that's not a normal thing to say."

"I can't even tell anymore what's normal and what isn't." I groaned sinking down in my seat. "Why's it so bad?"

"What would be the purpose in telling her that?"

"So she can avoid me."

"Why?"

"Because she thinks we're friends."

He was silent to the point that I wondered if the call had dropped. "What's wrong with being friends? Being friends with the person you love is . . . There's nothing better."

"That's sweet as hell and fucking annoying right now. And your situation is not the same as mine."

"It isn't."

I stared out of my windshield watching people wander in and out of the bar. On my chest grew the weight of everything I'd lost, my twenty-nine-year-old self shouldn't have been trusted to make decisions.

There was hesitation in Owen's words when he spoke again. "On the off-chance that this is helpful . . . you gave me advice once to swallow my pride. I don't know if I'm cool with you and Alicia, but I don't want you to keep regretting never telling her . . . whatever it is you need to tell her. Except for, 'I love you, stay away from me.' "

"I don't think that's helpful."

"Okay, pretend I didn't say anything."

He said goodbye when his fiancé called for him, and I drove home with my mind too loud to make out any one thought.

Putting my car in park under the carport, I took in the golden light filtering through Alicia's bedroom curtains. Just knowing she was in there—possibly naked—was enough to get me hard. I considered for a moment tossing pebbles at her window but decided it would probably land at creepy and not romantic. Then there was the issue that I'd become a stammering teenager, instead of the grown ass man I used to embody. There was a time, not that long ago, I had *some* fucking game.

Not anymore.

It only took a few minutes for me to get ready for bed, if Bliss hadn't demanded my attention the whole time it would have gone faster. But eventually I lay flat on my back, staring at the ceiling with my covers draped across me. Inhaling deeply, I caught the slightest whiff of a scent. And just like that the specter of Alicia was lying next to me, her hair a sprawling mess on the pillows. I was surrounded by her in my thoughts, in my memory, and in the smell of clove lingering in my bed.

Slipping my hand under the waistband of my joggers and pushing them down to my upper thighs, I gripped my hard cock, giving it one firm stroke.

My eyes closed in relief.

I couldn't satisfy my need for her, but I could quiet it. Pausing just long enough to pump lotion into my palm I started again. With each pull up and push down, my breathing grew heavier, my heartbeat pulsed in my grip, and I tried to recall exactly how she tasted. There was a rhythmic buzzing in my ear that called for my attention, but I stayed focused on the combination of reminiscence and fantasy playing out behind my eyelids.

Until I heard her throaty moan.

I froze mid-stroke.

Had I imagined it? Was I slipping that far into my mind?

All my attention was now outside of myself and focused on the buzzing—coming from the other side of the wall.

Fuck, I mouthed, throwing my covers off of me. Suddenly too hot.

Little creaks from her mattress carried through to my room, as well.

I pictured it. Her rocking her hips into her vibrator. I saw it in such clear detail it was like I was there standing at the foot of her bed watching. My cock twitched, and my grip flexed. I slipped my hand all the way off my head to push to my base. My toes curled. Everything drew tighter within me.

She groaned longer and a little louder. Cum dripped from my tip onto my wrist.

I wondered if she was watching something, or if like me, she just needed to think about us. Was she picturing my hands on her ass? Her tit in my mouth? My tongue on her clit? Was she wearing my shirt? Surrounded in *my* scent.

Give it back to me with your teeth marks in it.

Her moans and whimpers grew less controlled, her climax nearing.

Cum rushed under my palm as I grew closer too.

She cried out, a sound that rang in my ears before falling silent. I bit my teeth together, stroking hard—my bicep and forearm flexed.

It was silent in her room, until she let out a self-deprecating giggle. "God, I need to be fucked."

Cum spilled across my stomach in pulses. I sucked in deep breaths. Blood roared in my ears, but I could still hear her say, "That fucking man."

I needed to be the man she was talking about.

Chapter Twenty-One

Remi

"**Y**ou okay, Rem? You look rough." Nora paused in her filing to consider me.

I rolled my neck to loosen the tension in my shoulders. I'd slept like shit the past few nights. It'd been five nights since I heard Alicia through our wall. Ever since, I lay awake with my ears tuned into her as if she were a frequency they could pick up on like broadcast radio. Every creak of her mattress was torture, and my dreams were sweaty and hungry.

God, that sound.

Her sharp intake of breath before she cried out, the sound half caught in her throat mixed with the memory of her body taut in my arms, before slowly releasing and falling heavy to the bed.

"Hey." Nora set her paperwork down on the desk. "Are you good?"

Blinking, I realized I was glaring into space. I ran my palm down my face. "Yeah, just tired."

"You sure? Because if you're sick I can see if Brooks can come in. There's a nasty bug going around, and I'm already playing chicken with it by throwing a party tomorrow."

I only had the energy for a crooked smile. "Not sick, promise."

"Good." She gave one decisive nod as if everything was resolved. "You're still planning on being there, right? Elijah's annoying friend Seb will be there, and I fully intend to use you as a buffer between him and me."

"Seb is a good guy."

She only lifted an irritated eyebrow. "Olivia will be there with Anton too, and . . . Anyway, it'd be great if you were there."

She didn't need to elaborate. During our fundraiser in October, Brooks had taken his clothes off—not all of them, just his shirt—in front of the whole town. All because Olivia, Nora's twin sister, had flirted with him during the bachelor auction. And now, the town ran wild with speculations, even after she'd gotten engaged to Anton in December. It was a bit of a wild night, and Brooks could have just been feeding into the fun of it . . . or, and more probable, he had been motivated by something different.

Not that he was talking to me about it. I'd tried back when the engagement had happened, but he'd just grunted and walked away.

He could be very perceptive about other peoples' lives; less so about his own.

"I'll be there," I promised.

"Good." Nora considered her blood-red polished nails. "You really don't mind that Alicia will be there too?"

I snorted. "Nora, she's my neighbor. What difference does it make if she's at the party?"

I sounded confident and unaffected. Internally, just the mention of her name made my heartrate spike. She was an ache I couldn't relieve. I was desperate for any sign of her. Her clove smell had faded from my pillows, but from time-to-time I heard the whisper of her music through our wall or saw her red hair under a white stocking cap as she took Furgie for a walk.

She was everywhere, and it still wasn't enough.

No matter how I looked at the situation, I couldn't find a clear way forward. It was probably best that I didn't tell her how she haunted me, that I couldn't imagine just letting her leave and never being with her. Wasn't that the right thing to do? To not hurt her, again.

Every time I found resolve to keep my feelings to myself, I'd see her or think of her and my chest would feel too small to hold all the affection I had for her. There were three voices yelling in my head simultaneously.

I love her.

Let her live her life.

But the worst one was the quietest, *What if she still loves me too?*

Add on the obscene amount of jerking-off it took just to get through my day . . .

So, I had no idea what to do.

Nora narrowed her eyes at me. "If you change your mind and you need to bail tomorrow, it's cool."

"I'll be fine."

Just fucking fine.

My body knew Alicia was home before my brain did. The rush of adrenaline in my veins, and the tightening of my abdominals all in preparation of seeing her. I turned into my driveway, and she came into view walking up to her front door with Furgie on the leash lazily sniffing the mounds of snow, a little white clump stuck to the top of her nose. And walking by Alicia's side in a Carhartt coat was Emmett.

I didn't want to hate it, but I did.

The handle to my side door was cold against my fingers when Alicia called my name from the front porch. I gave myself a second to press my forehead against the thin wooden door and close my eyes. I was so close to avoiding the blooming relationship between the woman I breathed for and another man. While simultaneously, relief washed over me to hear my name from her lips—to have an excuse to talk to her. My brain was in a prison of my emotions.

With a deep breath, I straightened and moved around the corner of the building with a wave. I jerked my chin up in greeting to Emmett before letting my eyes fall on Alicia. She had a scarf wrapped around her neck and her bulky coat hid every single one of her curves, but my heart still skipped a beat and all the blood rushed out of my brain. I shoved my hands in the pockets of my scrubs hoping to disguise the semi I was suddenly sporting.

"Hey, what's up?" I asked.

"Give me just a second." She held up a gloved finger toward me before turning to Emmett. "Thank you so much for dropping those petitions off."

"Of course. I'll pick you up tomorrow for the party?"

My stomach twisted, and I grit my teeth.

"See you then."

He waved goodbye to me, pet Furgie, and took easy strides toward his pickup truck parked in Alicia's driveway.

She unlocked her door with the keys she pulled from her coat pocket. Rushing inside, Furgie shook off the cold and snow just inside the threshold. Alicia narrowed her eyes at the dog. "Gee, thanks, Furg."

I had enough good humor to muster half a smile, but there was no denying that I was in knots. Retreating to my apartment couldn't happen soon enough. At least seeing her and Emmett was enough to quiet two of the three voices in my head. It whispered a quiet guidance that I was finally ready to listen to.

It was time that I let go of all the baggage I carried around for her. The angst that sat heavy in my chest. The longing, like a magnet under my skin, urging me to hold her. The love that would have to find somewhere else to go.

"I have your shirt," she said over her shoulder as she kicked her boots off and headed for the laundry by the side door. "I washed it."

On the counter and table sat stacks of paper stapled together. On each page were line after line of signatures. "Are these the petitions you have all over town?"

I heard the dryer door slam. "Yeah," she said. With automatic movements she folded the garment as she walked toward me. "Now, I have the great task of checking them to be sure that we don't have any duplicate signatures, and there will be. But at least I'll know how close I am to getting an emergency vote."

"Do you think you'll have enough?"

She gave a lopsided shrug. "That depends on how many duplicates there are."

I wanted to offer to help, not because I was a good person fighting for the cause, but because I wanted to be around her. But there was that voice.

Let her live her life.

When I lifted my eyes to her face, she stood there chewing her lower lip. Her eyes darted from the papers, to me, to the refrigerator. But she didn't seem to have any intention of giving me my shirt with how she worked it between her fingers—pinching and rolling the fabric gently.

Her cheeks burned a soft pink before she asked, "Do you—would you like to hang out with me while I do it?"

A smile tightened the muscles of my cheeks—I only barely swallowed it back. Energy coursed through me, and I tried to reason with myself that it wasn't exactly the declaration of love I'd like to hear. But it was something. It was an excuse to stay. To hear her laugh. To watch her work. To be near her.

The place she took up in my chest grew too big again. I wanted to tilt her chin up, draw her eyes up to mine. Instead, I unzipped my coat. "That depends, what's the chip situation?"

The smile I'd been fighting spread across her face and finally she looked up at me. "Well in hand. Also, I have cupcakes."

"You're a way better host than I am."

She nodded. "I grabbed them hoping you'd hang out."

My stomach dropped out of my body as if I had stepped off a cliff. My pupils might as well have become heart shaped. I was a total sucker for her, an absolute sap. And all it took was her thinking about me even a little bit.

"Let me change out of these scrubs, and I'll be right back."

Chapter
Twenty-Two
Alicia

C hecking the signatures took longer than normal, though it was also less boring. Remi had offered to help, but I turned him down. I shouldn't have; it would have gone faster, but then he'd probably go back to his place. There wouldn't be any excuse for him to stay with me. He turned on *Archer* because he knew I had seen it before and it wouldn't be too distracting, but he was the real distraction in the room. At some point, Furgie had crawled onto his lap and was snoring gently into the crook of his elbow as he stroked the soft hair on top of her head.

It was so goddamn cute. I could have died just from the sight of it.

"Done," I finally said setting my pen down on the coffee table. I lifted my arms over my head and stretched back against the sofa groaning. Even though my eyes were closed I could have sworn that he was watching me. The caress of his gaze lingered on the slope of my neck and over the curves of my breasts. I was definitely imagining things. I'd been imagining things for a while . . . and my vibrator just couldn't do the trick. I got off, of course, and it helped with the constant . . . *yearning*—was that what this was? God, I yearned.

I needed to feel someone else's body on mine. It was almost compulsive, this reflex to reach out and touch. And the more time that passed,

I was becoming less certain that just anyone would be able to quiet the insistent noise in my head.

Remi was all I could think about. It was like the first time I'd seen him the semester before we actually met in that lecture hall. He was strolling across the courtyard outside of the cafeteria with a backpack over one shoulder and baggy jeans and vans on his feet. My mouth had actually fallen open. I positioned myself at that same window for the next two weeks just to catch another glimpse of him. It was in vain; I didn't see him again until the class we shared.

But I thought about him constantly, I concocted a personality for him that was quiet and broody—nothing actually like him. Yet somehow, the *real* him was better than my imagination. He was funnier, smarter, and he made an effort with my friends.

Now, the man he was over a decade later was better than my memory. I couldn't bring myself to think about anybody else; even Theo James interviews and movies couldn't distract me from Remi.

Lowering my arms, I looked over my shoulder to find him looking down at the sleeping Furgie, so I clearly was imagining him looking at me.

Maybe he didn't think time had been as kind to me as it was to him. Society definitely conditioned men and women to perceive aging differently; men got the privilege of getting hotter while women were supposed to do everything in our power to never age a day. It was bullshit, and I'd think less of him if he felt that way about me. That somehow I would be less desirable because time had passed, but him thinking that would also really hurt. I wanted him to want me as desperately as I wanted him.

God, this was torture.

This ill-advised crush.

"Does that mean we get cupcakes now?" he asked in a low rumble that shot electricity through my body.

"Is that all you've been thinking about this whole time?"

He grinned down at Furgie making it impossible for me to judge the tone of his expression. "I will not justify that question with a response."

"I guess you've been good enough to get a treat."

This time he smiled at me, and my toes curled under the coffee table in response. "I thought I was a guest. I didn't realize we were on the merit system."

"We're on whatever system I decide." I shrugged.

He narrowed his eyes at me. "Tell me more about these treats, are they from Country Grounds?"

"Yes, I'm kinda obsessed at this point. It's gonna be hard to leave that place when I'm done here."

"I mean, Chicago is no slouch on baked goods."

"That's true."

A muscle flexed in his neck as he swallowed. "You won't miss anything else about this place?"

It was as if he'd thrown out a fishing line baited with exactly the flavor I was looking for, and I must avoid it under every single circumstance. I pushed myself up to stand needing distance from the sharp cut of his jaw. "It's a cute town, but every place I go to for work is good. There's always something there to love."

He snorted gently moving Furgie onto the cushion next to him. Standing, he shifted his clothing that had clung in places that I craved more than anything my kitchen could store. "Yeah, but some places more than others."

Maybe it was because I'd turned my back, walking away from him into the other room, that made me brave enough to ask, "Would you ever move again? Or are you here for-like-ever?"

"Uh . . ."

I didn't dare turn to face him with how hotly my cheeks burned.

"If I met someone," he began, "and this wasn't the place for her, if she liked living in a city or something, I'd move."

Pulling the cupcake containers from the cupboard, I avoided his eye. "But it'd be a sacrifice, right? Like you really feel at home here."

"It would be a sacrifice I'd make willingly."

"So, you want to fall in love and get married and all of that?"

His response was so careful, words picked out deliberately. "I still want everything I wanted with you."

My eyes stung, but I refused to allow the feelings choking me to surface. He might have been able to clock that my smile was fake as I shoved the vanilla cupcake with chocolate frosting into his too broad chest—like really, what was the purpose in being so goddamn large? What was the purpose in saying all the right things *now*?

Anger consumed whatever else wanted to bubble to the surface. "Well, all I have is baked goods. I hope that's enough."

There was a sadness in the curve of his smile. "It's enough."

Ugh. Shut up.

But I didn't really mean it, and I reminded myself that it was a sign of my personal growth that I only thought it instead of screaming it at him or shoving a cupcake in his face.

"What about you?" he asked, catching me off guard. "What do you want?"

"To save this wetland and get home," I said ignoring his deeper meaning. It was true, but there was no denying "home" felt a lot more like him than Chicago.

With the cupcake in his hand, he ate about half of it in one bite. "Do you have more signatures to get?"

"Yeah, there were a lot of duplicates." I covered my mouth with one hand as I spoke around a mouthful of chocolate cake with chocolate frosting. "I just have this feeling like time's running out. Frost laws will lift soonish, and that's bad news for me."

He tilted his head in question.

"Because semi's are so much heavier, they cause a lot more damage to the roads, and while the ground is frozen there are certain roads they can't go on unless they have a special permit. Our lawyer at the capitol has heard that they're already applying for driveway permits and such. They must be getting pretty close to finalizing the purchase of the land, and I might still be able to fight the land's development at that time, but it'll be harder and a complete reset of my strategy. My limitations are set by how warm it gets and how quickly the ground thaws."

"And it's supposed to be in the forties next week," he observed.

I nodded. "My best chance of winning is changing the zoning before the property is sold. Even if I get the signatures, a vote still has to happen and pass. Time's running out."

I could feel it like a physical thing. A ticking in my chest, a bomb about to go off.

"Hmm." Remi swallowed his last bite. "Is there anything I can do to help?"

"Just keep helping me get signatures and whatever sway you have to win the vote when we get it."

"I don't know how much I could do there, but I'll do what I can."

"Please, Remi, you have to know how popular you around here. Hell, I hadn't even lived here for a day, and I was warned that my neighbor was *really* hot. I think the name was doc-too-hottie; not exactly a catchy nickname but it speaks for itself."

"Does it?" His eyes lit with amusement.

I rolled my eyes. "Does your ego need me to tell you you're hot?"

"Would you, for my ego?"

I was ready to say the truth, but I wasn't willing to do it with full sincerity. Stuffing the rest of my chocolate cake in my mouth, I mumbled, "You're like *really* hot."

"*You're* so hot," he retorted, laughing and shaking his head.

"You really think so?" I smiled back knowing my teeth must be covered with masticated cake.

"God, I do. You have a little frosting"—he gestured at the whole front of his face.

"Do I really? How could that have happened?"

He snorted. "It's a mystery. Here."

I froze when he reached for me, knowing how his thumb would brush my cheek. A shiver ran up my spine at his touch—then he swiped at my chin and nose sending my sexy-to-funny ratio too far in the funny direction for my liking. It left me wondering if the joke had been worth it.

"You wild animal," he practically growled, and I felt it through my whole body.

On the pad of his thumb was a dollop of frosting. He went to suck it clean.

"That's mine," I blurted out, clearly too fogged up on raw emotion, his attention, and lust to have any control over my mouth or actions. I took hold of his wrist in both hands.

Slowly, he shook his head from side-to-side while holding my gaze. "You always were food protective."

My body shook with laughter, but I didn't let him go. No one had ever made me laugh like he did, the pitch of it a bit brighter in my ears, it sounded good with his. His beautiful smile, wide and lined. The crinkles pressed deeper at the corners of his eyes. And his lips full and pink, they looked so soft. I remembered the press of his mouth.

I wanted it with a dizzying intensity.

My judgment hid within a cloud.

I leaned forward needing the clarity of his kiss. I'd understand everything if I could just rest my mouth on his. Taste what I'd missed for—how long had it been? It felt like an eternity. It felt like I had found this lost part of me. The part of me I left behind on that doorstep in the rain—

Gasping, I pulled back, releasing my grip and taking a step away.

Chapter Twenty-Three

Remi

Alicia flitted around the kitchen, throwing away the empty containers and grabbing a washcloth to clean her face of the last of the frosting. Her cheeks were bright red, whether from embarrassment or anger or some other emotion, I didn't know.

I looked down at the chocolate still on my thumb, and now that we'd almost kissed—that I'd almost had her mouth on mine—no other flavor would satisfy me. She went still when I took the two steps to the sink she was standing in front of. I wanted to run a comforting hand down her back, but I kept my hands to myself.

"Excuse me," I said.

She hummed and moved as far away from me as the counters would allow.

Watching the water wash over my skin, I asked, "You okay?"

"Of course. Why wouldn't I be?"

With an eyebrow raised, I turned to her.

Her exhale of breath depressed her chest and her shoulders fell a few inches, but she was still wound visibly tight. It was the smallest shake of her head that made it clear she didn't want or wasn't ready for us to discuss this further. She definitely wasn't ready to pick up where we left off.

Nodding, I looked out the window over the sink wiping a towel between my palms. It was dark. Of course it was dark, it was winter in Michigan—it was always dark. I missed the sun. The starless sky stretched over the cherry orchard across the road. The branches were twisted and sharp and empty. But there was life teaming under their bark. It just took some patience and then they'd be green and heavy with fruit.

If only patience could fix everything.

I gripped the back of my neck, only kind of wishing for death. "Well, I'm spent. I'm gonna head home."

"Good. Have a good night, thanks for hanging." She wouldn't look at me.

Alicia stayed tucked in the kitchen as I scratched the top of Furgie's head. She placed her front paws on my lower thigh, urging me to stay a little longer, but I was past my welcome. "You're a good dog."

I slipped my feet into my shoes and opened Alicia's door. I paused just before stepping onto our porch. For just a moment, I reconsidered leaving. I didn't want to leave us in this tension.

There is no "us."

The reminder was all it took for me to take that step out of her place. It didn't matter what I'd come to understand about myself and my feelings for her, she didn't want me here.

At home, I made sure Bliss's food and water was full. With an immense exhaustion that had more to do with my emotions than physical labor, I hauled myself up the stairs to my bed. I lay on top of my blankets unable to find the executive function to change into my pajamas. staring at the crack in the plaster of my ceiling, I listened as Alicia wandered from one end of her room to the other.

After a few minutes, her voice came through the wall, she sounded choked with the same emotions that made tears well in my eyes. "Hey,

Sadie, I need to talk. Can you just listen and not . . . throw my own advice back in my face?"

Her watery laugh at whatever the person on the other end of the call said twisted my heart so tightly that I rubbed my fist over it as if it were a muscle I could massage the ache out of. Moving as quietly as I could manage, I went back downstairs. Even though I could hear her didn't mean that I should. Just because I would give up some vital part of my body—which under scrutiny was pretty much every part of my body—to know what she was thinking and feeling, I didn't want to find out in a way that would violate her privacy.

I wanted her to come to me because she trusted me.

Instead, I stared up at the cracking ceiling of the living room trying to sort through my thoughts and feelings. Tears were just beginning to leak from the corners of my eyes into the hair at my temples, when Bliss chirped, jumping up on my chest. She lay down like a little bread loaf and purred. I stroked a hand down her soft fur. And little by little my eyelids grew heavy, weighed down by twenty pounds of fur and companionship.

Chapter
Twenty-Four

Remi

I almost backed out of Nora's party but decided that I'd just torture myself wondering. After a day of torturing myself wondering. It would be better to run into Alicia here than randomly somewhere else. It was bound to happen, and each time would build space between us and the kiss that didn't happen. We'd fall back into the easier territory we'd been in before last night. If I knew anything about her it was that she would clear the vibe; I'd just have to follow suit or . . . tell her how I truly felt.

Torture.

I'd decided that if I was going to leave my home, I was going to do it in my most comfortable attire. My black sweatpants and loose-fitting, gray T-shirt definitely fit the bill. I wore my glasses instead of my contacts, and my hair was tucked under a beanie. Brooks and I were sitting in silence, sipping our beers. I'd be nursing my drinks tonight. No need to be a lovesick idiot and drunk at the same time. I had zero faith in my ability to keep my cool around Alicia while under the influence.

Brooks was in his usual attire of a free T-shirt he got from some vendor and worn jeans. His baseball cap was pushed back and his unruly dark hair spiked out in every direction underneath it.

Olivia and her fiancé, Anton, still hadn't shown up.

Nora was in the kitchen, where the snacks were.

Sterling Strauss was the loudest person in the room—as was his usual—yelling over the chill music. Next to him, Ransom, his cousin, scowled. His ruddy eyebrows pulled together, and his jaw was set. I didn't think he actually disapproved of all of us, even though that was the messaging. I thought maybe his face actually did get "stuck that way."

It wasn't enough to deter Lindsey Miller from casting him hopeful looks.

I didn't usually sit on the sidelines of a party, but I could see the benefits. There was a lot going on around us, and I had a front row seat to all of it. It was kinda comforting, catching glimpses of everyone else not knowing what they were doing.

Hazel and Elijah stood a few feet away talking with Millie. While not trying to look at her too obviously, I wondered why I'd never tried to take her out on a date. She was sweet, and easy to talk to. And pretty, in a simple way, as if her features became more lovely the more I looked at her.

My phone buzzed in my lap with texts from Owen. He and Emmeline were at his parents for dinner.

> Owen: How's the party?

I glanced around, and my eyes automatically landed on the front door—always looking for Alicia. I couldn't help shaking my head at my own stupidity.

> Me: Just amping up. It's still chill at the moment. But shit usually doesn't hit the fan until Olivia shows up.

> Owen: Not your shit, though.

I snorted.

> Me: No, my shit is fine.

> Owen: Will Alicia be there?

> Me: She should be.

My eyes flicked to the still closed door. Her arrival would be met with relief that I could stop anticipating it, and tension that my attempts to be friendly had backfired so spectacularly.

I wanted her.

I missed her.

I loved her.

I was so annoyed with myself.

> Owen: You sure your shit isn't gonna hit the fan?

No, I thought, but I typed out, ***I'm good, man.***

I hadn't told him about last night. Three little dots came and went on the screen until finally, he sent, ***That's great. I just kinda don't believe you.***

Owen had been my best friend for years, and especially through the divorce. It didn't surprise me that he saw through my attempt at a brave face.

"Can I sit here?" Lola pointed to the cushion between me and Brooks. Her large dark curls draped over the shoulders of her jade-colored sweatshirt. I hadn't seen her since the other night at Benji's. I smiled a greeting up at her.

"Mmm," Brooks grunted jerking his head toward the empty spot between us.

"Yeah, of course." I shifted closer to the armrest. It was still a tight squeeze. Her thigh and arm pressed against mine, and she held her shoulders tight taking up as little space as possible.

I swung my arm over her head to drape it across the back of the sofa. Shifting my back toward the armrest as much as I could, I tried to give her room. "Is this okay?"

"Yes, thank you." Her shoulders loosened. "That's so much more comfortable."

There was a breath of awkwardness that my nerves were too fried to deal with. I needed some small talk and quickly. "So, what's been going on with you this week?"

She blew air through her lips. "Work is already busy for tax season."

"Will it be a less intense spring?"

"No, I think it means that my busy period will just be longer."

"So, I should schedule with you now." It was a lame attempt at a joke, but we were keeping it light.

A sardonic smirk fit onto her face, and she shook her head. "Yes, that's exactly right."

"Understood." I grinned down at her, but I still noticed the front door opening.

Emmett held it for Alicia. The room shifted in her direction, gravity pulled me toward her. The lights in the room dimmed as all the energy was sucked into her. She was heat and power. She was the pull that I kept resisting.

Her eyes met mine then landed on Lola tucked into my side and under my arm, before darting away.

Fuck.

Shit, meet fan.

Chapter
Twenty-Five

Alicia

The edges of my vision darkened, and my cheeks burned. The only thing that saved me from marching across the room to give Remi a piece of my mind was my job. My very important job. I couldn't quite list all the reasons it was important at the moment, but I did know that it was, and that I loved it, and that I desperately didn't want to fail at it.

He looked cozy with his arm around another woman—which he had every right to do. But also, and I meant this from the bottom of my feet to the top of my head, fuck him.

For making me confused and jealous.

For making me cry.

I thought he'd grown out of being a piece of shit, but apparently he hadn't and that was fine, because fuck him. It was humiliating to fall for the same asshole twice. I thought I had grown out of him too.

"I need a drink," I said to Emmett, hoping that I sounded less frantic to him than I did to me.

He placed his hand on the small of my back and led me through the room and into the kitchen. The smell of chili powder and cumin came from a crockpot on the countertop.

Just inside the door, he paused with a hand on the wall by my cheek, his body creating the semblance of privacy. "Ya all right?"

"Of course. Why wouldn't I be?" I sounded almost convincing.

He rubbed at the back of his neck. "I might feel a bit . . . ya know . . . if I were you."

Yeah, I know.

"I'm okay," I lied. "Thank you for checking."

I wanted a drink in my hand to keep them from clenching, and if it had enough bite to it I could blame the tears stinging my eyes on that. How had I let Remi in enough to hurt me? Again?

Emmett took a step back, letting his hand slip back to his side. With a little jerk of his head, he led me further into the room. "What do you wanna drink?"

"Um . . . something strong."

He nodded giving me a sympathetic quirk of his lips.

The kitchen looked like a grandma's circa 1990, which it was. When he'd revealed that they party at Nora's grandma's from time-to-time, I'd needed some convincing to stay. But he'd pointed out that it would be the best place to get to know people and promised to take me somewhere else if I was uncomfortable. Now, the party's location had nothing to do with how uncomfortable I was.

I followed him to the middle of the kitchen with its oak trim throughout, blue countertops, and a wallpaper boarder depicting ducks in a pond over and over. Nora stood with her arms crossed over her chest, the alcohol on the island directly behind her. She lifted an eyebrow at a man about Emmett's height with thick, dark hair. The man was dressed casually but everything fit *perfectly*. Just anyone might assume that his jeans and T-shirt took as little attention to put together as Emmett's, but there was no way.

I knew a fuckboy when I saw one. Though, I was possibly giving myself too much credit, because I hadn't clocked Remi as one.

While I was dealing with my own drama, there was still enough room inside of me to hurt for Sadie. She was sticking to her plan and ghosting her own fuckboy. But I knew it took something from her every time he texted.

But this stranger had a cocky purse to his lips, and a glass of amber-colored liquid over ice, pinched between two fingers.

Judging body language alone, Nora held all the power here.

He turned his head, and his grin grew warm and welcoming. "Emmett."

They shook hands before pulling each other into a quick hug.

"Seb, what's up?" Emmett answered.

"No complaints. How are the horses?"

"They're good. Lots of work."

Nora tilted her head, and I got the sinking feeling that she could see the emotions I was hiding. "Alicia, thank you for coming."

"Happy to be here." I pointed to the ducks in the pond. "I'm weirded out it's your grandma's house."

She laughed. "You should be. It's a weird group that decides this is what we want to do."

"Why do you?"

"Nostalgia? Every time my sister comes back to town we do this. Grandma loves it, because one of these people are going to notice something needs to be fixed and they just show up and take care of it. In the spring, Ransom noticed the gutters were all messed up, and this was the first year Gram didn't have water in her basement. It's a good trade off."

"All right, that's sweet."

"It is."

"Alicia?" Seb asked extending a hand to me.

It was warm in mine, but I didn't completely trust the polite gesture. "Seb?"

"Yeah. Sebastian."

"I'm sorry, I should have introduced you—" Emmett began but Nora interrupted.

"Should you, though?"

Seb's hazel eyes sparkled, clearly delighted. "Don't mind her, she doesn't know it yet, but she's in love with me."

I snorted. "Obviously."

Nora reached between Emmett and Sebastian to pull me next to her. Turning her back to them, she gestured to the alcohol bottles and mixers arranged on the island. "What do you wanna drink?"

I considered my options, maybe it was the house reminding me of my pre-bar days, but I shrugged and said, "How about rum and coke?"

"Classic." She spared Emmett and Seb a glance over her shoulder as she grabbed a red solo cup and started heavily pouring the rum. "He's Elijah's business partner."

I didn't have to ask her who she was referring to. I glanced at her out of the corner of my eyes. "Are you into him?"

She fought the smile tugging at the corners of her lips. "No. But he's entertaining too."

"You have your fun, girl."

"I will. He shows up with Elijah every once in a while."

"Who's that?"

"Hazel's boyfriend." She pointed into the other room, where Hazel stood next to a man with wavy chestnut-colored hair. I didn't know what was more shocking, how hot he was or how hot Hazel was. She used to be the quintessential nerdy college student, frizzy ponytail and all. But as she grinned up at her boyfriend, she looked confident and empowered.

"Good for her," I said.

"Yeah, he's great. Total looker. But he's the lucky one. Hazel's the best."

Appreciation filled my chest as I accepted the drink Nora held out to me. I used it to gesture between us. "You and me? We're gonna be friends."

She rewarded me with a completely sincere smile. "We are."

Noise carried through the closed kitchen door where the group had been smoking on the back porch, it quickly grew louder and moved closer. Excited cries and laughter filtered into the room, drawing attention before the door had even opened.

"Here comes drama." She lifted her cup to her lips and took a big drink just as the door flung open.

A woman who looked a lot like Nora stepped through with a crowd behind her. But where Nora wore an old hoodie and her curly hair in a bun this woman wore a curated outfit of a flowy long skirt and cropped Fall Out Boy T-shirt under a puffy blue coat that ended at her waist. Her makeup was immaculate and her hair was shiny and straight past her shoulders.

"It is way too quiet in here!" she exclaimed.

From the living room people cried out, "Olivia!"

In the chaos, I snatched my drink and snuck out of the back door. There was a lone mercury light buzzing from high up on the house and a sheet of stars in a dark blue sky. The cold pressed against me, shutting down the persistence of my mind to wail and angst. For just a moment, I closed my eyes and let the relief and quiet sink in.

I considered my options and whether it was time to call it a night already. My gut reaction was to move past the emotional turmoil and stay. But the more I considered it, the less I felt that I had the energy for it.

Then the door I had just exited opened and closed, revealing Remi.

A new surge of energy burned through me riding on outrage.

The cold was a distant memory.

I came to stand at my full height.

"What the flying fuck, Remi?" I demanded. "Why are you out here? Did you follow me? What do you want?"

"I just want to talk." Drenched in light, every detail of his face was completely visible.

"About what, exactly? What could we have to talk about?" I gestured between our chests. "Whatever this weird relationship we have, this whole thing, let's just be done with it. Let's go back to never speaking. We don't even have to wave hello to each other. I will be leaving soon, hopefully, and we can just put this in the past with *all* of the rest of it."

"I don't want that."

"I am done, Remi." My voice broke as I said his name, but I was too far gone to be embarrassed by it. "I am *disgusted* with how I have acted, and with you, and how you are making me feel. That you can affect my feelings at all. I am *disgusted* with myself."

He sighed, running a hand down his face.

I clenched my jaw fighting back my tears. "Aren't we divorced? Isn't this supposed to be over with? You're not supposed to be able to hurt me, anymore."

His chest sank like all the air had been knocked out of him. A crease dug deeply between his eyebrows as a muscle flexed in his jaw.

"Why did you come out here to say *nothing*?" I asked. "Go back away. We'll pretend like this is the old days—you give me the silent treatment, and I'll pretend like it doesn't bother me."

I expected him to glare at me or accuse me of being wrong for my feelings. Instead, he looked at me with eyes full of intense emotions but none of them were anger. "I don't want to do that."

"Then string together more than five words, because I. Am. So. Fucking. Over. This."

Chapter Twenty-Six

Remi

Alicia's back was lit from overhead, outlining her in silver and hiding her face from me, at least the fog had cleared from my glasses. Her fists were balled tight at her sides. I'd followed her out to the back porch, but now I second guessed if that was the right choice—she clearly wanted to be alone. And I was the last person she wanted to see. I was here now, in a conversation that was nothing but thin ice. Just the mention of her leaving was enough to turn my blood cold.

She was justified in her anger—it hadn't happened yet, but I was still nervous that she'd attack the way she used to—a remark too far past the argument only to cut me.

And worse, that I'd fall back into my old shitty responses.

There was no way that I was letting that happen.

"I fucked up," I said. It wasn't enough after the long silence that had stretched between us.

"I'm gonna need you to be more specific, because as far as I can tell, we have been fucking up for weeks. First, we almost"—she looked over each shoulder then hissed—"*kissed* last night."

I felt slightly better that she was acknowledging it.

"And I'll be completely honest, this whole situation is fucking with my head even more than I thought it would," she admitted. "I get that

I practically kicked you out of my place last night, but it was . . . Remi, what am I supposed to do with all of this? Nothing makes sense." She pointed a finger directly at my face. "But *then* I walk through the door, and you're all cozied up with someone else. And I feel like the psycho, because, yeah, of course you are, and there's no reason for me to be upset—"

"I'd be pissed," I mumbled, but she didn't stop.

"Do you even get how goddamn thoughtless all of this is? Or how embarrassing it is to want to cry or scream at you in front of people? Which isn't entirely fair, God, because I'm sure I'm sending you mixed signals. Like, what the fuck am I even going on about right now?" She blinked up at the sky, the tears welling in her lower lids caught the light and twisted my heart in my chest. "You are not responsible for my feelings, but what the fuck is going on?"

I crossed my arms to keep from pulling her into me. A sickening weight grew in my gut as her breathing grew shallow as if she was fighting back tears. This was the opposite of what I'd set out to do when she'd shown up in this town. I hated to see how tightly she held on to her tears, while knowing that my actions in the past had proved to her that I wasn't safe to be vulnerable in front of, or with.

I hated to make her cry.

Scowling, I parceled through everything she had just said looking for the correct place to start. I needed to prove to her that this wouldn't be like it used to be. I wasn't the same. That we could work through our issues and come out the other side unscathed.

She wiped the heel of her hand across her cheekbone at a tear that had overwhelmed her efforts to keep it in.

"Lola is just a friend," I said, regretting that it sounded exactly like something a guilty person would say.

"It doesn't matter."

Taking a step closer, I insisted, "It does. Even if our past relationship wasn't what it is, last night . . . almost . . . I wanted it so badly."

Want it.

Alicia was all I could think about.

The words were right there, insistent, but her face was still submerged in shadow making it impossible to know if now was the right time to completely open up. There was never going to be a perfect moment, but a better time than now was a possibility.

Even if loving her felt so obvious that I couldn't believe she couldn't see it.

I would tell her exactly how I felt. Before she left for Chicago.

Her leaving loomed over me, this unknown deadline with all its ramifications. And she'd be gone. I hadn't been lying when I said I'd follow her back to the city; I didn't care where I was as long as I was with her.

"I'm sorry." I pulled my beanie down further over my forehead. "The sofa was small, and I was trying to give Lo more space. I'm sorry I didn't think about how it would look to you when you got here."

Alicia let out a humorless laugh. "Why would you? You're single."

"Because I watched the door ever since I got here. I can't stop looking for you."

"Remi," she whispered. It could have been a warning. It probably was.

I swallowed, my heart skipped a beat as adrenaline coursed through my system, gearing up to give her an apology that should have happened five years before. "And I'm sorry for that night." She grew unnaturally still, but I kept going, "You were so brave, you were doing something that I was too afraid to do."

The image of her dripping from the rain clutching the pages of our damp divorce paperwork superimposed on her blacked-out outline.

"I was so cruel. I regret it every day, even more now that I've met you again."

For a moment, neither of us moved or spoke. I didn't even breathe. It was as if I'd grown thin as tissue paper; she could tear me up without even trying.

But then, she closed the space between us. The slightest pressure of her weight pressed into me, and she rested her cheek against my sternum. I wrapped my arms around her, and she shivered. She still held herself tightly, leaving our embrace one-sided. But that was fine.

God, everything was good.

She was real. She fit perfectly. This was more than I could have ever dreamed.

"Where is your coat?" I asked, resting my chin on the crown of her head.

"You're one to talk."

"I hate when you're cold."

"But not when *you* are?"

"I'm not all that concerned about me."

"I am." Her admission was barely audible. It could have disappeared in the crunch of snow, but in the still silence I heard. I had to squeeze my eyes shut to the emotions those two words flooded through me.

She nestled her cheek against my sweatshirt. "I should get back in there. I know it's weird, but I am here for work."

"I can help."

I didn't let her go, and she didn't pull away.

"Where does all of this leave us?" she mumbled into my chest.

"I hope better than where we started."

"Does it? I'm so confused."

I wasn't confused. Not at all. I had the utmost clarity.

Chapter Twenty-Seven

Alicia

"Hey." A guy wearing a baseball cap moved to Remi's side and gestured toward me with his can of Bud Light. "Is that actually your ex-wife?"

I was technically in a conversation with a few people about the local high school basketball season, but I wasn't invested by any means. I'd overheard people asking about mine and Remi's past relationship a couple of times, so I knew what was coming next. No matter how loud the party got, I could always hear Remi's name or, God help me, his voice. It had been a few hours, and more drinks than was wise, since my conversation with him. My feelings were still a little frayed, but staying at the party had turned out to be productive. When he'd said that he would help me, it hadn't been empty words.

"Yeah, we used to be married," he said. "Have you met Alicia?"

He didn't wait for the other man to answer before calling out, "Leese, do you have a sec?"

I gave him a smile over my shoulder and held up a finger in the universal sign of, *one minute*. While I removed myself from the group I was a part of, I overheard Remi talking to baseball-cap-guy. "You know that state land you hunt on?"

"Yeah."

"They're trying to sell that off and put in an amusement park or some shit."

"Goddamn, really?"

I was walking the few feet to Remi as he nodded, gravely. "She's here to stop it."

He gave me a big smile that made me curl my toes. I had to force myself not to lean into his side, that hug outside was still fresh in my mind—how it had felt like the entire world was reduced to him and me. The security. The gentleness.

Were my emotions frayed? Or was I resisting the one thing that felt the most right?

After introducing me to baseball-cap-guy, Brian, a local construction worker, Remi stayed just like he had the two other times he'd initiated this conversation, acting as a built-in hype-man.

"So, what is this petition supposed to do?" Brian asked.

"To give the opportunity for the county to vote on rezoning the land to protected status," I explained.

"You'd still have to win the vote, even if you get enough signatures." He was a bit standoffish, and I couldn't get a good read on how to appeal to him. I hoped my connection to Remi would be enough.

"I would, but it would also stall their progress and give me more time to let people know why this land is so important."

A crease formed under his lower eyelid as he considered me. "Yeah, no thanks."

Remi straightened. "You won't sign the petition?"

"Nah."

"Can I ask why?" I took a sip of my drink to keep from sighing.

"I don't like telling people what to do."

"But you're not telling *people* what to do," Remi argued pinching the frames of his glasses and pushing them back on his nose. "You're telling the Michigan government what to do, which you do every time you vote."

"Nah, I'm good."

"That's bullshit, man—"

I placed a hand on his forearm to cut him off before he created more tension between Brian and my cause. "No, it's okay." To Brian I added, "I hope you change your mind. I would love to talk more extensively, if you have any questions."

After a tense few seconds, Brian walked away claiming that he needed a fresh drink.

I raised an eyebrow at Remi. "You can't bully people into signing."

"That mother fucker—"

Laughing, I shushed him. "Not here."

His eyes locked with mine. "At home, then."

My stomach flipped, and my cheeks warmed. Remembering that home was Chicago came as an afterthought. One that couldn't hold up to the feeling that the city was just where I lived, but *home* was wherever Remi was.

"Yeah," I agreed.

The musical selection did not have a through line. In the past three songs, we'd listened to Brand New, Jay-Z and currently the whole party was screaming out the lyrics to "Nothin' On but the Radio" by Gary Allan. Well, not the whole party. The first chorus Sebastian obviously didn't know the words, but he was catching on and singing it directly to Nora. Which I suspected she didn't *actually* find annoying. With each drink she consumed, it became more clear: She liked Seb.

Brooks also didn't sing along; he swayed with a beer in his hand. One time I thought maybe he glanced at Olivia, but she was grinning up at her designer-styled fiancé, Anton. He reminded me of an Abercrombie & Fitch model from the aughts. When he took off his coat in the kitchen, I expected him to be shirtless. His lips were always parted. I didn't know how eyebrows brooded, but his definitely did. He was the total antithesis to Brooks, but when Olivia looked over her shoulder it was always in Brooks' direction.

I could not figure out the dynamic there.

I was on the drunk side of tipsy. So when someone suggested that we play Never Have I Ever, I loudly said, "I'm gonna need a full cup for this."

The room full of practical strangers laughed, and I wondered if that was a bit too far. If playing the game at all was a bit too far. There was a line between integrating into the community and losing credibility.

"I'll play." Olivia shrugged.

"Looking for an excuse to stay sober," Nora deadpanned.

"Fuck you, Nor." Olivia laughed, but behind her Anton's expression grew harsh. She took in the party goers ending at Brooks. "This could be fun."

A woman with a sharp-edged chin-length bob scowled at the group. "Are we seriously playing a drinking game? No one else thinks we're too old for this? Nostalgia can only be justified so far."

"Remove the stick from your ass, Janet. You don't have to play if you don't want to," Nora suggested.

Seb lifted his drink just above shoulder level. "All right, I'll go first. Never have I ever had a one-night stand."

Hazel gasped. Her boyfriend threw his head back laughing.

While Nora and I exclaimed in unison, "Bullshit."

I had officially drank too much. I did not know this man, and I was acting like a fool. This was the kind of game I would normally remove myself from, but I felt Remi's attention like a weighted blanket around my shoulders. I was too curious to walk away.

"It's true, I haven't. Sex gets better the longer you're with someone. Why would I do it only once?" Sebastian explained.

"Not always," Olivia said. Her eyes widened and she started blushing as soon as the words were out of her mouth.

"Lucky, that's not the case with us." Anton clasped her hand and kissed her knuckles.

Smooth, dude.

"To one-night stands." Nora held up her cup then took a hearty drink.

A good percentage of the room followed suit, including Remi and me.

It was followed by, "Never have I ever been naked in public."

I drank.

Remi didn't.

"Never have I ever had sex at work."

Hazel took a discreet drink through her straw. Elijah tried but failed to hide a shit-eating grin.

I could barely hear Remi whisper, "Tell me it was your office."

"You already know too much," she whispered back.

I snorted.

Her brown eyes met mine for the first time all night.

"Good for you," I said, trying to lighten the mood between us.

She narrowed her eyes in response. "Never have I ever stayed out until six in the morning."

Heat bloomed on my cheeks, but I took a drink. The statement was clearly for me, as I flashed through memories of him calling or texting wondering where I was. But that was the whole point of those nights. To make him angry and worried. To push him past the point of sullen petulance—provoking him.

Remi glowered at her in warning, and his jaw set.

Someone else started saying the opening phrase, but Hazel cut them off. "Never have I ever had a breakup so bad that I almost failed my senior year vet finals."

The room grew quiet enough that we could hear Sterling mutter, "That feels really specific."

My whole face burned, and I was absolutely positive that I was the brightest shade of red. This was definitely not a good look for me—not for my job or whatever it was that was going on between me and Remi. He crossed his arms over his chest and shook his head once. Elijah rubbed a hand across Hazel's shoulders, and she settled into him as if realizing what she'd just said—how she'd laid our past out for other's consumption.

She turned her face down to her feet. The whole interaction felt very different from the quiet girl I used to know, but then we all changed. I had, but she didn't know that.

I didn't feel like playing anymore, but I couldn't remove myself without it being noticed, so I stayed waiting for the attention to shift away from me.

The silence that followed only lasted for a few seconds before Olivia's too bright voice called out, "Never have I ever . . . dated two people at once."

Nora drank, but at least three different people said, "Define dating."

"Dating," Olivia repeated.

To my surprise it was Emmett who spoke up to clarify. "No, but is it non-exclusive relationships or is it two people who think that you're monogamous and you're actually cheating?"

"Let's go with open relationships. Cheating is just depressing," Nora confirmed, but I caught her fleeting accusatory glare cast toward Anton. If she killed him tonight, I'd help her bury the body.

"Never have I ever . . ." Nora began, "had a threesome."

Remi drank.

Despite my mood, I was wildly curious.

"Brooks?!" Olivia gasped.

His shoulders remained relaxed, one finger hooked in his belt loop. "Hm?"

"You *have*?"

He nodded.

"Shit, Brooks," a guy to my right said appreciatively.

"Was it you, a guy, and a girl? Or you and two girls?" Olivia's dark brown eyes were huge.

He tilted his head toward his shoulder. "Yes."

"Which one?"

"God, Liv, both. He's had more than one," Nora explained.

Olivia's lips formed into a circle, before she swallowed. I could have thanked her for shifting the attention from me so efficiently.

"Brooks, do you fuck?" asked a bald man.

Using her cup, Nora gestured toward a quiet Brooks. "He's drank more than anyone else in this room"—she jerked her chin toward Sterling—"sorry, I forgot you were in here."

He smiled. "Nothing wrong with a little experience."

The broad-shouldered man with red hair standing next to Sterling rolled his eyes.

"Never have I ever had sex outside," Seb said.

Remi's eyes pinned me—a memory hot and bright in his midnight blue depths. Cold rain falling heavy on our rain-soaked clothes, as we kissed and moved together. My shorts and underwear in a pile on the ground, his around his thighs. Neither of us lifted our drinks. We both knew. And it was ours. Only ours.

Just us.

A reminder that we had been good together, so good. And that we were good now. It didn't matter what anyone else thought of whatever we were, or of me. It was us that mattered.

Even with how sloppy and careless we had been with each other's hearts I'd go back there now, even if it meant living through everything that would come later. I'd take the pain to have the good.

I'd do it all again with him.

Chapter Twenty-Eight

Remi

L ife was funny. A few weeks ago, I wouldn't have believed there was a possibility of Alicia walking up to me with her cheeks flushed from alcohol, and saying, "You're sober, right?"

"Yeah."

"Do you mind taking me home? I can ask Emmett, but it looks like he's having fun—"

"No," I interrupted with an eager break in my voice. "I'm ready to go."

The pink of her cheeks deepened as a smile split across her face. Her amber eyes glinted. A gentle breeze could have knocked me over. I was a goner, and maybe she knew. And maybe she was gone with me.

I handed her my coat from the backseat of my SUV to drape backward across her shoulders while we waited for the engine to warm up enough to kick heat through the vents. She nuzzled it up to her chin. I gripped her headrest to look over my shoulder as I backed up. Within seconds we were on the dirt road that would lead us back to our place—places.

It was good to remind myself that I still didn't know what she wanted from me. I couldn't attach myself to her if this wasn't what she wanted. My heart ached at the thought, but I'd survived the loss of us once. I could do it again.

"So, Hazel hates me," she said, drawing me out of my thoughts.

I winced. "That was so fucking shitty of her."

Alicia raised an eyebrow. "Doesn't mean she didn't have a point."

"And what exactly would that point be?" I asked, my tone harsher than it should have been—I was angry at Hazel, not Alicia.

"That she has reason to be protective of you about me."

"She refuses to acknowledge that I was an asshole to you too."

She chewed on her lower lip, a crease formed between her brows. "You almost failed your exams?"

"I didn't, though. This will probably shock you, but I didn't handle our divorce well."

"Yeah." She turned to look out the window. "Me either."

The conversation went dry, while my thoughts were preoccupied by a future where she'd fit me into her life. It at once felt insurmountable to pass this distance our divorce created, and at the same time, she was so close to me. I knew her. It was so easy to fall into these conversations, because we fit. I just didn't know if that was enough for her.

"Can we listen to something?" she asked, breaking the silence again.

I grabbed my phone off its dashboard mount and handed it to her. "Sure, the passcode is my birthday."

"Oh, free access to your phone, how very brave of you." She punched the four digits without hesitation.

"I don't think there's anything exciting in there that you haven't seen before."

"You keep your own nudes?"

"Sometimes it's hard to get the angles right," I admitted.

She snorted. "So true."

Imagining her sending me nudes had me trying to discretely shift the fit of my pants. Damn sweats left nothing to the imagination.

She put my phone back on the mount, the beginning chords of Sufjan Stevens' *Illinois* album began playing through the speakers. "What about the ones that are sent to you?"

My cheeks warmed. "I don't keep them. It feels wrong if we're not in a relationship."

For a moment, she was silent as she tapped a finger on her armrest. "So, you don't have mine anymore?"

The pause between her question and what should have been my denial was too long; in the silence she read my admission of guilt.

She gasped, angling toward me in her seat. "You do, don't you?"

"I couldn't delete them."

"*Them*?! There's more than one?"

I drove one handed with the lower half of my face hidden behind my other hand, as if it would make the embarrassment easier to manage if she couldn't see it. "Not a weird creepy amount. I haven't looked at them in years."

"Oh, I have a creepy amount of you."

I straightened, completely forgetting any of this was awkward. "You do?"

"Apparently you're a nudes prude, so probably."

"Is it like a full frontal, or just dick pic?"

"I've got you at every angle."

Yeah, there was no hope for the pants and concealing my growing hard-on.

"Am I the only exception to your rule in here?" Her voice trailed off as if the answer was of no consequence.

"You're the only exception everywhere."

There was a beat of silence, before she asked in a voice barely louder than the music, "Why couldn't you delete them?"

I wouldn't be able to delete the Mona Lisa either, was too corny to say, but it was the first explanation that came to my mind. There was more than naked pictures in my password protected photo album of her. A photo of her laughing so hard I knew in real life no sound was actually coming out. One of her rolling her eyes at me. And the last one, was of her sitting on the beach with her eyes closed as the breeze blew back her hair, the setting sun casting its rays on her skin. The freckles on her nose the same color as her vibrant hair.

Yes, the pictures of her naked were sexy and made my body ache for her, but they revealed different elements of her as well that I couldn't just . . . delete.

"If I showed them to you, you'd understand," I finally said.

I turned into my driveway and parked under the carport. The windows in our units were dark. We walked to the front porch, and I followed her up the steps. My coat hung too big off her shoulders. I held my arms tight across my chest waiting for the fog to clear from my glasses enough to see her properly. On the plus side, the cold had distracted my body enough that I was no longer posting a tent.

There were the muffled sounds of Furgie barking and whining behind Alicia's door.

I leaned back against the railing as she released Furgie into the front yard.

"Aren't you freezing?" she asked, but it couldn't dispel the weight in the air around us.

"Yeah," I answered.

She pulled her phone from her pocket. "Why don't you go inside?"

Despite the cold, my palms began to sweat. But loving her in secret was killing me. I couldn't keep skating around the truth indefinitely; I had to at least nudge us toward her knowing—toward me saying . . .

"Because you're not in there," I mumbled, scraping the toe of my boot at a patch of ice clinging to porch.

"Oh no," she breathed.

My blood ran colder than the air freezing my lungs. I forced myself to look up at her, even though it felt like she'd dug my heart out of my chest with two syllables. I thought I was prepared for my heart's potential to break, but of course I wasn't.

Who could be?

What was the point of her flirting? Was this some elaborate revenge scheme? To convince me to open up, just to reject me in the end.

As soon as I saw her stricken face illuminated by her phone screen, all my feelings of pain and anger turned into concern. "What's wrong? Is everyone okay?"

She tilted her head up and swallowed. "Fuckboy lawyer."

"Fuckboy?"

"Uh, not mine. Sorry. He's in Lansing. He's helping me." Rubbing the back of her neck, she lowered her eyes back to her phone. "He just texted me and Sadie, '*It's going to shit. I'm sorry, ladies. They're getting special permits to begin excavating before the deal is even finalized. I'm still fighting it, but it's not looking good.*'"

"So, what do we have to do?"

Her mouth hung open for a minute as if searching for words. Finally, she shrugged her arms heavy at her sides. "I need all of my signatures now."

The quiver in her voice was torture. I ran a hand down her arm, not that I could feel it through the baggy fabric of my coat. "The permits will take a little while, right?"

"Depends on how tight they are with a judge. But I'm so close. The petition is almost there."

Furgie climbed the stairs and shook, sending clumps of snow flying. Alicia ducked her head, and I angled my body to block her from being hit. The tap of paws on carpet registered somewhere in the back of my mind, but I was too preoccupied by the pinch of Alicia's brows and the defeat in her eyes.

"We'll get this figured out." I brushed a loose strand of hair behind her ear. "No one is more devoted, and creative, and . . . you don't give up. You'll figure it out. We're not done. We'll get everybody rallied, and fuck . . . I don't know, Leese, but we're not giving up. Not when this means so much to you. Not when it's the right thing to do—"

Whatever I was going to say exploded into nothingness, along with everything else I'd ever known, because Alicia's mouth was on mine. My entire existence began and ended right there.

Her hands fisted into the hair at the base of my skull. I took hold of her ribs and pulled her to me like I was the moon finally able to plunge into the ocean instead of pushing it away. The taste of her, so rich in my memory and real on my tongue. The whimper at the back of her throat. The feel of her body hot against mine. She was my entire world.

Chapter
Twenty-Nine
Alicia

G iving in had never been so good. No other craving I had ever surrendered to had been this fulfilling. Remi was the richest chocolate cake the day before my period, and the drippiest ice cream cone on a hot day. It was too good to even care if I'd regret it later. I stood on my tip toes, needing to get closer, taste more. His arms around my waist kept me from falling on my ass, my arms around his neck couldn't pull him in tight enough. I hooked a leg around his waist as if I could literally climb him, before long he took hold of both of my thighs, and hoisted me up.

I was not a small woman.

He didn't even grunt when he did it.

His coat was bulky around my wrists. I couldn't get my hands on him like I needed.

And God did I need it.

Somewhere in the back of my mind a voice whispered about consequences, but I drowned it out by rocking my hips against his erection, hard and thick inside his sweatpants, sending electricity throughout my entire body. He groaned moving his hands up to cup and squeeze my ass.

My logical mind knew this was dangerous—that my feelings for him were more than lust and something like friendship. It was clear that there were only a few scenarios where this didn't end up with me, and him, brokenhearted. Again.

But I still needed more.

And less.

Less clothes. Less distance. Less logic.

What was the point of logic anyway, when no amount of it could have kept me from right here pressed between his body and the interior wall of my apartment? And logic never felt this good. Nothing had.

Only him.

He pulled his glasses off of his nose and tossed them somewhere. Then he moved to kiss my neck, and I sucked in a sharp breath at the scrape of his teeth.

"Please tell me you have a condom," I gasped.

His hands slipped under the opening of his coat to cup my breast in his big hand, brushing his thumb back and forth over my already sensitive nipple. "In my wallet."

"Get it."

"I will."

"Now."

He tugged the neck of my top down running his mouth over the swells of my tits. My body was all sensation, completely incapable of any other function than soothing the desire burning through me. Could I die from not getting fucked fast enough? Logically, no. But as I'd already established, logic didn't know shit.

I took two handfuls of his full light brown hair and pulled. His eyes were foggy and lusty. His lips were swollen and wet.

The ache between my thighs throbbed.

"Now," I demanded.

He shook his head from side to side. "We just started."

"I can't fucking breathe I need you so badly."

"Not yet."

"Remi," I warned.

"Alicia." He kicked the door—that I had completely forgotten existed—closed and set my feet back on the floor. But my legs were no longer load bearing, and I would have fallen over if he hadn't set two stabilizing hands on my hips. When he decided I was no longer a fall risk, he lowered to his knees. "I have missed every inch of your body, and until I get my mouth on all of you, I won't be fucking ready."

He unbuttoned the closure of my jeans, his mouth peppered kisses along the soft bottom of my stomach, each press of his lips to my skin sent shivers down my spine.

"That's a lie. I just had your *readiness* pressed against my stomach."

His shoulders bounced, and I felt him smile against my naked inner thigh. "Readiness," he repeated.

My head fell back against the wall, accepting that he was going to take his time and that I probably would survive. He pushed my jeans down to bunch around my ankles, until they couldn't go any further past my boots. He bit down gently at the top of my hip then kissed the sting away. My knees were growing less reliable again.

"Fuck," he said, his mouth inching closer to my center. "You could convince me I'm dreaming."

I snorted. "If this was a dream, my boots and pants would have magically disappeared."

He peered up at me, his eyes dark with want. His fingers curling around the waistband of my underwear and pulling them down. "And your shirt."

"Not your coat, though?"

With a slow side to side, he shook his head. "I like seeing you in my things."

"I've got something you can try on"—the last word hit a high pitch I didn't know I was capable of before it cut off, because Remi's tongue had slid between my lips and passed over my clit. I smacked my hands on the wall looking for something to hold on to. My pants kept me from widening my stance to balance, and I grabbed Remi's shoulder. With his hands on my hips, he urged me to the table, and we both laughed at my shuffled steps. Toeing the heel of my boots, I kicked each of them off.

He pulled the ends of my jeans off my feet leaving my wool socks, which felt a bit unsexy, but also the floor was cold so I kept them on.

His hands were warm as he opened my lips before running his tongue up my center, and we both moaned in unison. I took hold of his hair in one hand, burying my fingers in the soft strands. He rocked his head back and forth in a slow rhythm. Each pass drawing me tighter. My fingers tightening. My knuckles against his scalp.

He groaned, and the vibration of it rippled through me. His movements grew faster, the pressure firmer.

My orgasm came in a gentle wave. I curled over the top of his head, my legs twitching.

Placing sweet kisses on the inside of my thighs, he gave me time to catch my breath.

When I had finally unfolded, and loosened the hold I had on his hair, he looked up at me with his dark blue eyes. "In my right-hand pocket is my wallet."

"I thought we just got started," I remarked, my throaty voice failing to convey the snark I intended.

"I might have overestimated how long I can hold out."

Chapter Thirty

Remi

A licia pulled my wallet out of my coat and handed it to me. I unfolded it to pull the condom out of its spot in the deepest pocket behind my credit card. The whole time she kissed my neck and ran her hands down my stomach until they slipped under my waistband causing my fingers to fumble. I had to give up entirely when she gripped my shaft and pumped one stroke. My balls drew taught, and precum dripped onto my boxers.

She turned her face to me. I bent to kiss her. The taste of her pussy mixed with the taste of her mouth, and the flavor made my head swim. She was familiar and new.

I tossed my wallet somewhere and took hold of her ass with one hand. Squeezing, I savored the way she spilled between my fingers.

With hurried movements, she pushed my pants and boxers down until she could slip her wet cunt up and down the side of my erection.

Her head fell back with a sigh, and I let my forehead drop to her shoulder watching where we met, her reddish-brown hair glistening at her mound's deepest point. I licked my lips wanting to taste her again, if not for the insistent throb in my cock.

"Fuck," I groaned, taking hold of her hip to keep her rocking.

The foil packet between my palm and the tabletop shifted, drawing my attention to her fingers tugging at it. She tore it and rolled the latex down my shaft. Her eyes met mine as she placed my head at her entrance.

I wanted to tell her how, what, I was feeling. That she was everything to me. That my heart had been lost, and it'd found home as soon as I'd found myself face-to-face with her all those weeks ago.

But her amber gaze was molten.

And I couldn't find the ability to speak.

Instead, I pushed into her inch-by-inch. Her head fell back, her mouth open in a silent moan. I slipped out almost completely pushing in again. Every muscle in my body tightened to keep my pace slow.

I knew nothing—not what this meant to her. If this would be just once or . . . Kissing her, making love to her, might be the worst act I could do for the preservation of my heart, but I'd deal with the fall out later. I would do anything for this. It didn't matter what condition she left me in, I would do this again. And again. And again.

"I needed this," she whined.

I could only nod.

"You have such a hold on me." She hugged her arms around my neck. "Nothing feels this good."

Cupping her jaw, I urged her head up to kiss her again. To fold our bodies, and souls into one. I never wanted to be separated from her again. I wanted to capture this. Us.

An old wound in my heart cracked open, and I begged silently, *Let her love me too.*

But I was willing to accept anything to feel her cunt tighten around my cock and hear the sounds she made as I plunged to her very limits over and over. Our movements grew more urgent. Her fingernails dug into the flesh of my upper ass. I snaked one of my hands up her shirt to pinch and circle her nipple. Her gasps spurred me, and I heard the tear of her bra before I even realized what I was about to do. I didn't have time to offer to replace it before I lowered my head to pull her breast into my mouth.

She cried out, and I felt the ripples of her orgasm around my cock. Waves crashed over me. Her nipple fell from my mouth with a pop, and I fell atop her, gasping into her hair.

We were silent except for our panting breaths. She finally spoke, saying, "I cannot believe this table was able to take that."

I chuckled. Pushing up to my elbow, I looked down at her. I'd have to pull out from inside her, and deal with the condom soon—just not yet. "Sorry about your bra. I didn't mean to rip it."

Her pleased smile grew slowly. "You did, though. You ripped the shit out of it."

"I kinda lost my fucking mind."

Her eyes darkened. "Me too."

I opened my mouth, ready for those three words to fall out, but chickened out at the last moment. "Do you want to come to my place, or should I go grab my box of protection and come back here?"

My soul left my body in the breath of time before she spoke, and uncertainty flickered across her face.

But then, she ran a palm along the stubble of my jaw. "Your bed's more comfortable than mine."

"Good, I miss my pillows smelling like you."

A naked Alicia lay draped across my chest, her hand rested in a gentle fist right above my heart. We'd tossed my blankets and sheets, and we'd need them eventually, but for now our bodies were hot and slick with sweat. My pulse slowly lowered to its normal rhythm. For the first time in weeks, my brain was silent from the constant need for her. In its absence was peace.

Not even the aching desire for her to love me could whisper in my ear. Not when loving her was enough.

"Oh!" She shoved my chest.

I startled, opening my eyes that I hadn't realized I'd closed.

"Shit, sorry, were you asleep?" she asked.

"Just somewhere in between." I shook my head, a lopsided grin forming on my lips. "What's up?"

"You can help me brush up on my euchre skills."

"You're thinking about euchre right now?"

"I was invited to play with the club next week."

I winced. "There's no 'brushing up on your skills.' Those women are going to annihilate you."

Her jaw dropped and her eyes widened. "I can hold my own with a deck of cards."

"No. Leese, you don't know these women. It is the town's hub for information, you should go, but they're gonna wipe the floor with you."

She shook her head, a blazing fire in her eyes.

"Okay, listen to me." I ran a hand down her hip. "I know you're good. You're a top-notch strategist and a solid euchre player, but these women are . . . brutal. They're gonna wreck your shit. It's not your fault. You don't stand a chance, Leese."

"I do not accept defeat."

"I know you don't."

She ran her tongue across her front teeth. "Have you ever been?"

"Women's only club, but I've heard tale."

"Been the subject of conversation there?"

"I've gotten that impression." It wasn't a big deal, everyone in town had been the focus of the club from time to time.

"What's the big rumor about Remi these days?" The tilt of her lips was doing things to my brain—and the rest of me too. It was an invitation to play with fire.

"Right now?" My voice dropped a bit lower in a way I knew she liked. I took hold of her hip easing her onto her back—hypnotized by the bounce of her tits. "That my neighbor is my ex-wife."

Fuck. I loved her laugh.

Her eyes were alight and mischievous. "Wouldn't they love to hear about *this* development?"

"I know I'm fucking in love with it," I said. Kneeling between her thighs, I ran my hands up her sides.

She trailed her touch along the front of my thigh to my pelvis, then to the strip of light brown hair trailing down to my already hard cock. "Jesus Christ, look at you."

"Look at you," I groaned, taking her breasts in both of my hands. Her hair was a mess splayed across my bed. The pale freckles on the bridge of her nose matched the few on her shoulders. She was all slopes and valleys. So soft, and strong.

Lowering, I trailed kisses down her shoulder. I had placed my mouth on every inch of her. It'd only made me hungry for more.

"Remi?"

Something in her tone made me freeze. I turned to face her; her lip caught between her teeth. "Yeah?"

"Can I see the photos you have of me?"

I snorted, completely caught off guard.

"I'm pretty curious," she admitted.

A twinge of vulnerability twisted in my gut, but I agreed, "Show me yours, and I'll show you mine."

"Deal." She rolled onto her stomach to army crawl to the edge of the bed, and I took the opportunity to give the full curve of her ass a playful slap. First she gave a surprised gasp and then sighed as I kneaded her sensitive skin. I placed a few more kisses on her spine. Every movement was a distraction, but eventually we lay side-by-side on the bed holding each other's phones.

"These are pretty tame," she observed. "I'm not even naked in some of these."

I placed a kiss on her temple, and muttered, "You make me into such a pervert, I can objectify you no matter what you're wearing."

I could hear the smile in her voice as she said, "Oh yeah?"

"Bring that puffy coat of yours next time, and we'll act out one of my fantasies."

Laughing, she rested her head on my shoulder and continued scrolling through my album of her.

She had fewer photos of me than I did of her, in them I was younger and skinnier. Less wrinkles on my face. Less meat on my bones. I envied that version of me, but not because of his youthful looks, but because he still had her. But that version of me could never have ended up back here sharing a bed with her. He was frankly too dumb to figure his shit out.

I would never return to him even if somehow I was offered the opportunity.

In one of the pictures, my old robe hung open, with a mug of coffee in my hand tipped so far it was about to spill. A surprised intensity in my eyes made it clear that I was watching her just past the camera, and whatever she was doing to herself had me completely hard. Another, she had taken as I leapt off a rock naked, a deep blue sea extended behind me. It was a good picture, and my thighs and ass were flexed. My thighs had always been her favorite feature of mine. The last was a video, in it I was jacking off telling her how badly I wanted her with me. My grip on my cock was white-knuckled, and the muscles of my arms and shoulders were bunched. A vein strained against my neck, as I fucked into my hand.

"I need you," I had groaned. *"I love you."*

She went unnaturally still. I could feel the tug of her growing distant, like a wire around my heart tightening. All I wanted was to suspend this moment between us, to keep us here—clearly feelings weren't the way to do that.

Not yet.

"Do me a favor," I said, handing her the phone.

She lifted her eyebrows, and her nipples grew taught as I knelt between her thighs again, this time lowering to my elbows. "Watch me lose my fucking mind over you, while I get you off."

"Oh, fuck, Remi." Pink grew in her cheeks, and she licked her lips. Her knees fell open wider.

I grinned up at her devilishly. "Hit play."

She did. I lowered my mouth to her sweet cunt, teasing her closer and closer to her orgasm while the younger version of myself said, *"I love you,"* over and over.

Chapter
Thirty-One

Alicia

"I'm being completely shut out here," my firm's Michigan lawyer, Jamison, said through the phone pressed to my ear.

I looked up at my kitchen ceiling; wheat stalks were etched into the frosted light fixture from the fifties. My jaw was too tight, but I couldn't convince it to relax. Through clenched teeth, I said, "So, it's signatures or bust?"

"And fast. I don't know what kind of deals are being made, but almost everyone I had on board to put the property to public auction has flipped." He sighed. "They won't even schedule a meeting with me."

If not for spending most of my nights with Remi, this week had been shitty. That damn party was all anyone wanted to talk about. I'd bring up the wetlands, and then drama from the weekend would become the subject of conversation. Everyone throwing out same questions and speculations as everyone else. *"What did Olivia mean about sex not getting better?" "Where did Nora go?" "Could you believe Brooks?"* And those were just the speculations about people I actually knew.

It was so annoying.

Muffled sounds of a Counting Crows album carried through the wall dividing my place with Remi's. An album I knew by heart because it was Remi's favorite. He listened to it when he felt pensive and needed comfort. What was he thinking about? Was it me? He was on my mind like a patch of earth that had been worn away by a thousand footfalls. It wasn't a path intended to be there, but it always followed the same twists and turns until he was my destination.

I needed to stop wondering about him and focus on my job. Time with him was . . . so good. Terrifyingly good. He made me feel less alone as all the work I was doing came to a halt—falling apart into so many pieces. I couldn't find these last few signatures, only people who had already signed. Every night, he came back with a few more names on the petition he was circling around, and I'd combine it with mine. It was helping, just not fast enough.

Every night I found myself wrapped in his arms, soothed by his touch, and comforted by his words.

I needed to get this job done. At least if I was able to force the emergency vote, I could postpone going home for a few more weeks to shift gears and drum up support.

An excuse to stay here longer. To save this land where so many species called home.

To stay with Remi.

To have more time to figure out exactly what was going on between us, because it wasn't just sex. But could we really be more? He'd said for the right person, he'd move. Did he actually mean that? Could I be the right person *again*?

Then there was the strange settling in feeling, like I could stay here. My job was on location a couple weeks out of the year, and everything else I could do remotely.

If there was a way to a future with Remi, it'd probably be less of a disruption for me to stay.

Was I absolutely unhinged for even wondering any of this?

Was there anything more unhinged than love?

"How's progress going on your end?" Jamison asked.

I groaned. "Slower this week."

"We need public outcry. We need those signatures, and the emergency vote—"

"Are you just giving up at the capitol?" I demanded.

"No." His deep breath carried through the speaker. "I just want to prepare you. I was appealing to these politicians as individuals, so if they've been swayed. I've got very little else."

"I'll get the signatures," I promised. "I've got a social event tonight that could make a difference."

"Good."

"Is there anything else?" Finding Furgie curled into the corner of the sofa, I scratched the top of her head goodbye.

"Uh . . ." It was uncharacteristic for Jamison to sound unsure, and I waited for whatever he was going to say next. "Have you talked to Sadie?"

I rolled my eyes. "Yeah, why?"

"I'm having a hard time getting a hold of her."

"No, everything I've sent her has gotten a timely response."

"Gotcha. I'll check again."

We hung up, and I felt a combination of protectiveness and guilt. Because I really wanted to tell him to leave Sadie alone. But also, I hadn't told her yet about things between me and Remi. And it'd been a week. She and I had talked.

She was going to be so pissed at me.

The music went silent on the other side of the wall. I considered for a moment if I had enough time to knock on his door and maybe make out for a bit. Which was alarming, because I had just given myself a pep talk about getting my head into my work.

Instead, I grabbed a couple of snacks from my kitchen and let Furgie out to go to the bathroom. It felt a little weird not to text Remi that I was leaving, but we didn't live together and we weren't dating, right?

Ignoring that last thought, I jogged out to my car.

It wasn't a far drive. The sun was setting, but it was dark enough that the streetlights were lit. Euchre club was being held at a woman named Ginny's house. I parked in the elementary school's parking lot across the street and grabbed the tray of cookies I'd ordered from the local bakery, Bake This Way.

Through the door, I could hear women talking and laughing. I raised my hand to knock, then let it fall. My energy was all off. I needed this night to be a huge success.

Hyping myself up, I plastered a smile on my face and knocked.

A woman with short white hair answered the door. With a wide welcoming smile, she said, "You must be Alicia. I was wondering who'd be knocking on the door, most everyone just walks on in like they were all raised by wolves."

My smile felt more genuine. "I am Alicia. Are you Ginny?" I asked.

"That's me, sweetheart. Come on in out of that cold."

"Thank you so much for having me."

"The pleasure is mine! Especially, when you're carrying all of those cookies—that snickerdoodle might as well have my name on it."

"We *could* set these down in the kitchen and share them, *or* we could hide them in your closet and eat them ourselves."

She threw her head back and laughed. "Tempting, but I get hangovers from too much sugar these days. I wouldn't be able to move tomorrow."

"I guess we'll have to share them then."

"Not that snickerdoodle, though."

"Nope. That one's yours."

She led me through the hallway lined in family photos that all looked about ten years old. As we neared the kitchen the voices grew louder.

Taking the tray from me, Ginny called over the noise, "Ladies, this is Alicia."

I spotted Deb Creger and Mrs. Simons from the library right away, as well as Nora. But she seemed to be the only other woman our age there. Everyone else was closer to my parents' ages.

Waving a hand, I returned the group's greeting. "Hello! I've been warned that you are ruthless euchre players, but I promise to hold my own."

"We'll go easy on you if you tell us about Remi," a woman with thick black eyeliner yelled.

I'd been expecting a comment, especially after he'd warned me, but I hadn't expected it so soon in the night—or so publicly. All of the blood rushed to my face, and I struggled to keep my smile while wishing my complexion didn't go bright red when I was embarrassed.

You cannot fail tonight, I coached myself. But a charming, lighthearted response was not coming. Instead all I could think was, *He dicked me down real good last night.*

I glanced back at Nora, not sure if she knew anything about me and Remi. We weren't exactly going anywhere together. Were we public? Or was this a secret fling between me and, let's face it, the love of my life?

"Why haven't you ever offered that to me, Trish?" Nora joked. "I know Rem, I'll spill to win a hand here or there."

I didn't know what deity I invoked to bless Nora and any of her potential offsprings, but I hoped they heard me. As far as I was concerned, she was St. Nora of Grand Ridge, patron saint of havin' a bitch's back.

The playing began, Nora and I were teamed up and the first to be eliminated. The whole game took half as long as any game I'd ever played before. It was brutal. I would not be telling Remi that he had been right.

We grabbed plates of snacks and sat on the sofa to watch everyone else. "Is it always like this for you?" I asked.

She paused with a chocolate chip cookie halfway to her mouth. "Oh yeah, I've never made it to a second round. But while my grandma is out of town I come so I can pass on all of the *news*."

I snorted. "How is Stella?" I asked, recalling her name from last weekend.

"She's . . . a lot, but she's great. She'll be home sometime in April, so you'll probably meet her."

My stomach dropped. "It's kinda looking like I don't have that long."

A line pressed between her eyebrows. "What do you mean?"

There was no reason for me to hide how poorly everything was going, and some urgency might help undecided people take action. After I'd finished telling her everything, Nora stared into space for a few seconds. I picked up snippets of conversations around us, my brain not processing any of them.

"How many more signatures do you need to get an emergency vote?" she asked.

"Maybe a hundred, which in terms of signatures isn't a lot but . . ."

"There aren't a ton of residents," she completed my thought. "You have the petition with you now?"

"Of course, I'm just waiting for the right time to pull it out."

She held her hand palm up. "Let's have it."

With some hesitation, I pulled the clipboard with the thousands of signatures I'd already collected from my bag.

Nora took it from me, standing, and spoke over the sounds around us. "Excuse me"—she extended the clipboard over her head—"you all know why Alicia's here, right?"

Most everyone nodded.

"Good." She scanned the room, looking like a war commander about to rally the troops for battle. "Ladies, we've got some wrongs to right."

Havin'. A. Bitch's. Back.

By the time I left Ginny's, I had a few more signatures. But more importantly a few more people committed to my cause. And hope, a little more fucking hope.

Chapter Thirty-Two

Remi

B enji's was packed, but mellow. It was more of a gathering of people who were just bored of being inside this late in the winter, but they were bored together. Brooks, Hazel, and I sat at a table waiting for Nora and Alicia to join us after euchre club.

Hazel and I had talked about the night of the party where she couldn't even pretend to be polite to Alicia, and how I did not fucking like that. I understood Hazel feeling protective, I had felt the same way when her boyfriend had blindsided her with a breakup a couple of months ago. When Hazel had gotten back together with Elijah, I'd been skeptical, and I wouldn't have described myself as warm toward him. But I wasn't an asshole.

Obviously, I wanted my friend, and boss, to be decent to . . . whatever Alicia and I were to each other—we were avoiding conversations about relationship labels and the future. The stress of it was not making me better at being patient with Hazel's attitude.

The conversation had gone *okay*.

I kept the details of me and Alicia vague, which was easy to do since they were vague.

"It's not your job to decide who deserves to be around me and what can or cannot be forgiven," I pointed out.

"That's not what I'm doing?" Hazel replied.

"Then what are you doing?"

"I don't have to like her."

"Of course not, but that's not what I'm asking of you."

She sighed and nodded.

She had apologized, but I was still skeptical of her sincerity.

Which I would tolerate as long as she wasn't mean.

I was also a bit on edge because it would be the first time Alicia and I were hanging out in public, and I wasn't sure how we could act. Being alone with her, touching her, it would be really hard to pretend that I hadn't relearned the paths of her body.

Then she walked through the door, and I knew without a doubt I wouldn't be able to. Her clothes were appropriate for a casual hangout with the grandmas of the area—loose sweater that ended just above her hips, and wide legged jeans. But the hints of her body underneath was enough to drive me crazy. Her hair was in a high ponytail—all girl next door and sporty.

She scanned the room until her eyes met mine. My heart almost beat out of my chest at the triumphant smile that filled her face. I shifted in my seat, placing my elbows on the table, my own smile absolutely conquering my face.

"Yeah?" I asked as soon as she was in hearing distance.

She nodded. "I got 'em!"

"You did?!" A shiver ran through my entire body, a mixture of joy, and pride, and love for this woman who wanted nothing more than to make the world a better place.

"I did," she practically squealed.

My chair scraped loudly against the polished cement floor. "You did!"

She fell into my open arms, her face hidden in my neck, and I knew she was fighting back her tears.

"I knew you would," I whispered, emotion thick in my throat. "I knew you would."

Pulling back, she dabbed under her eyes with her ring fingers. "I didn't."

It was a testament to my restraint that I didn't kiss her then. Her eyes shone with unshed tears and her cheeks were pink. Her eyes darted to her left, which was how I realized we had an audience the size of the bar. The world around us was like a mosquito buzzing around my ear, irritating and I couldn't swat it away. This wasn't my moment, anyway.

"Let's celebrate." I pulled the chair next to mine out for her. "What do you want to drink? My treat."

"I'll get the next one," Nora offered.

But Hazel shook her head.

For a moment, anger spooled in my gut. It would be very hard to forgive her if she ruined this night for Alicia.

It washed away when Hazel said, "I'll get it."

It was by no means an absolution of Alicia's and my past, or even an acceptance of what we might be. But it was good as hell of her to extend the gesture.

"Feels like I should offer too," Brooks added, lifting his beer in a lazy cheers.

"Thank you all, so much." Alicia beamed.

Shortly after, I returned to the table with the drinks. Nora and Alicia were recounting the evening. The card game had been forgotten as soon as Nora made her announcement, and phones were pulled out—instructions on how to use various phone brands hollered across the room as some of the technologically impaired struggled.

"Then cars started showing up," Alicia said, excited energy coming off her in waves.

Apparently, when the matriarch of these families asked, or told, their children and grandchildren to show up and sign a petition, they did.

"It was the most powerful thing I've ever seen," Alicia added. Under the table, she pressed her knee to my thigh.

The space between our two chairs had grown too far. I'd probably only be satisfied if she was in my lap. I could bear it; this couldn't be worse than the past couple of weeks. At least I'd had an excuse to hug her. At least I had the press of her knee. At least I was close enough to smell her clove-scented shampoo.

"Lily even pulled up to sign." Nora crossed one leg over the other and looked at Alicia. "What did she say to you?"

She pursed her lips and narrowed her eyes at the ceiling in thought. "Something like, *the one that got away*. It was the weirdest thing. I don't even know her."

I rubbed my hand across my jaw. "Remember the appointment I had before Furgie?"

She gasped. "That was *her*? Remi, that woman is dressed in red flags."

Holding my hands out, I said, "I never. I didn't even encourage her."

"You didn't even get to play any euchre?" Hazel asked, changing the subject which I appreciated.

"One hand," Alicia and Nora said, practically in unison.

Alicia must have caught me smirking, because she rolled her eyes.

Hazel tilted her head toward Nora in false sympathy. "That bad, pumpkin?"

Staring down at the tabletop, Nora shook her head. "It's violating every time."

"It was as much a slaughter as you said it would be," Alicia admitted.

I squeezed her knee under the table, letting my hand rest there longer than necessary. "There was nothing you could do."

"The patronizing is really soothing the sting of it."

Giving her my most sanctimonious expression, I nodded. "I know."

"Hey guys." Lola walked up to our table, her bulky coat wrapped around her shoulders.

We greeted her, and Alicia smiled, but I could feel her tensing. I knew it had more to do with the embarrassment of feeling jealous of someone else, than it had to do with Lola herself.

"Bet was supposed to come, but Melody got sick right as she was walking out the door. Is it cool if I hang out with you?" Lola asked.

"Of course." Nora looked at the tables around us, then pointed. "There's a chair over there."

"Great, be right back." Lola turned to grab the empty seat.

There was room for her at the end, but I had the excuse I'd been looking for. I hooked my fingers on the underside of Alicia's seat and tugged, pulling her as close to me as I could. Her thigh relaxed against mine, and I had to drape my arm across the back of her chair. She flicked her eyes up to mine with a flash of desire and promise.

Nora and Hazel were distracted with getting Lola settled.

Not that Alicia and I went completely unnoticed.

Brooks' eyebrow twitched, but he didn't say anything.

"Now there's plenty of room," I whispered in Alicia's ear.

"I like it better here, anyway." Her fingers splayed across my leg, before resting on the inside of my thigh. And I wondered if it was too early to take her home.

Chapter Thirty-Three

Alicia

"You're getting handsy, Miss It's-Fine-I-Can-Handle-A-Fifth-Drink." Remi didn't make any efforts to stop my hand drifting down from his chest to his stomach. He leaned lazily against the wall outside of a storage closet. I'd grabbed his arm, pulling him around the corner like an old vaudeville hook, pretending like this hidden hallway was privacy and not just the illusion of it.

"I'll make a deal with you," I offered. "I'll keep my hands to myself if you start getting mouthy."

"What exactly does that mean?"

I shooshed him as his laughter made his voice louder.

"Get that mouth on me, baby," I said in mock sexiness. It was meant to be funny, but also I wanted him to take my words seriously.

"Here?" he asked, his voice pitched low.

I bunched the cotton of his shirt in my fist and went up on my tiptoes to scrape my teeth along his jaw. He gripped my hips. The sheer size and strength of his fingers had me wondering just how much we could get away with in the dark. A growl rumbled in his throat right next to my lips.

"Let's get you home," he said.

My back stiffened. Pulling away, I searched his eyes. "Would it be that bad for someone to see us?"

His thick, long eyebrows shot up wrinkles pressing into his forehead. His thumbs drew soothing circles on my pelvis. "No. Not for me."

"Then kiss me."

"I don't know if this is what you actually want or if you're just drunk."

"I always want this," I admitted.

He urged me forward until my stomach was pressed against the ridge of his growing erection. With slow intention, he lowered until his lips brushed mine. My eyes fluttered close. My heart fluttered into a million little pieces—tickling down my spine. His hand slipped to splay wide between my shoulder blades, deepening the kiss. It was a tender urgency. This call and respond.

Every little movement he made drew something out of me, something that longed to be seen in the way he saw me. To lean into the support within the circle of his arms. To whisper, *I love you*, against his soft full lips.

He pulled back, exhaling deeply then pressing a kiss to my forehead. "I wanna take you home. Now."

"Okay."

Neither of us moved, because to leave was to untangle our limbs and I just couldn't yet. Instead, I wrapped my arms even tighter around his waist and rested my cheek against his chest. His heart thumped a steady beat that I could set my clock to.

Kissing my temple, he peeled out of my hold. "I'll go grab our coats. Be right back."

We snuck out the back door to the parking lot, and I retrieved my bag with the petition, double checked that my car was locked before sliding into the passenger seat of his SUV, as we pulled out of our parking spot. Benji's supported cars staying overnight if it meant sober drivers, which

I loved. It wasn't exceptional for a small-town bar, but I'd gotten out of the practice of free parking. I did not miss paying for parking.

Counting Crows' *Time and Time Again* played on the speakers quietly, and I wondered, again, what had Remi in contemplation.

"This album has been playing a lot," I said.

"It's a good one," he responded.

I resisted in pushing him further, but just barely. "It is."

Remi rested his hand on my leg as he turned onto the road. It was good how natural it was to be touched by him. I hummed " . . . Baby One More Time" by Britney Spears off key, smirking at the memory of Remi doing the loosely ass smacking dance move she did in the music video earlier that night. This time, I hadn't had to watch him smile and dance from across the bar, I'd been in the mix with all his friends.

This place was pulling me in, and it'd be easier to resist if not for Remi.

"Your Spears' impersonation is pretty fucking good," I mumbled.

He chuckled. "Yeah, I've got all her moves."

"How did I not know?"

"I was such a scared little boy when you knew me. It's a lot more fun to not be afraid of whether or not I'm man enough."

"Oh, baby"—again, with the fake sexy voice—"you're man enough."

"I know that voice is a joke, but it's fucking working."

"God you're easy," I retorted.

"Are you calling me a slut?"

"Would you be into it if I did?"

He tilted his head, then said as if surprised, "I don't think I would."

"Holy smokes, did we just find a turnoff?"

"Well, I've had my slutting it up time in the past, but definitely not in the last few years." He glanced at me out of the corner of his eye. "I think I just like you."

Warmth unfurled in my stomach, tickling through me. Electricity zinged down my spine. It was anti-climatic and an absolute understatement to say I liked him back, but I did anyway. He squeezed my leg as we pulled into his driveway.

Laying my head back on the headrest, I closed my eyes. "I might have to go back to Chicago, so I stop drinking so much."

I didn't think anything of the quiet inside the car, filled with only the sounds of the wheels on the gravel coming to a halt, until Remi cleared his throat. "Might have to?"

"Hmm?" I asked opening my eyes.

"You might have to go back to Chicago?" He put the car in park, and turned in his seat to meet my eyes, but it was too dark for me to read anything from them. "You don't know for sure?"

My jaw hung open for a few moments as my brain sloshed drunkenly back to the words that had come out of my mouth. "Well, I mean, I will be staying . . . for the vote . . . you know?"

He looked out the windshield again, a muscle flexed in his jaw, and he slipped his hand off my leg to turn the car off and grip the steering wheel in both hands. "Gotcha."

I rubbed my suddenly sweaty palms on my jeans. The blood rushed in my ears. "Are you okay?"

"Yeah," he said, his voice a bit too light. Forced. "I'm okay."

The option to drop this conversation was right there, he was offering it to me. And I was scared to say what I had to say. I strung the syllables together saying them as quickly as I could. "Wouldyouwantmetostay?"

The words were thin, they'd break under any pressure, but there was no going back now.

He cleared his throat and swallowed. "I want you to do what you want."

There was a thud that rang inside my head, like a hammer on a nail. Like a coffin sealed. A door slammed shut. I was too shocked to speak, to think, to run away inside of my apartment. I'd been afraid to say anything out loud, but I had actually thought . . .

"And I want to be there with you, wherever that is," he continued, dragging me out from under the darkness of my thoughts and feelings with such forcefulness I was dizzy. "I wasn't lying. I still want everything I wanted *with you*. I'll go to Chicago. I'll stay here. I'll move to the fucking moon, if *you're* there."

"I don't want to go to the moon," I said around a watery laugh.

"Me either, but I don't care where we are."

"I don't either."

"I love you." His smile looked so light he could fly away. I felt like I might fly too.

"I love you, too," I whispered.

There was no way to know who moved where or kissed who first. We weren't and then we were. Slipping our arms free of the seat belts across our chests to hold and touch and pull closer. With nothing held back, nothing unsaid. Nothing but endless possibilities with the man I loved desperately.

Remi kissed along my jaw and down the slope of my neck to the tops of my breasts, his hands cupping to give him better access. I remembered that we were steaming up the windows of his car, at the same time that I recalled the barrier of trees all around the property. No one could see us.

"Remi?" I breathed.

"Hmm?" He answered. Undoing the top button of my sweater, he pulled it to the side to scrape his teeth on my nipple over my bra.

For a moment, I forgot what I was going to say before recovering. "If we went to the moon"—he cut my words off with the flick of his tongue, and I gasped.

He glared up at me through his light brown lashes. "We're not going to the moon."

"But you said—"

"I know what I said." I could feel him smile against my skin as he repeated his attentions to my other side. Heat pooled at my core, my hips shifted instinctively. One of his hands trailed to press between my thighs. "I'll get you to the moon."

"Are you talking about your ass?"

His shoulders shook, and he looked up again and hummed *Major Tom*.

Chapter Thirty-Four

Remi

Alicia and I poured through my front door, kicking off our boots and tearing off our coats like it was a race to get naked first. I could not stop grinning. It'd taken until the car was almost the same temperature inside as the outside and the windows were completely steamed for us to pause long enough to go in the house.

Our clothes were discarded in piles on our way to the stairs; her sweater over there, my jeans here. Her bra near the bottom of the stairs. My boxers halfway to the second floor. We discovered each other with our mouths and hands. Her naked body completely flush against mine, as I pressed her to the wall just outside of my bedroom—kissing her as if our lives depended on it. As if now that we'd said the words, I could really truly give her my love.

She rocked her hips rubbing her slick heat against my thigh.

My cock throbbed and precum dripped between our bellies.

I filled my hand with her tit, flicking my thumb over the hardened nub of her nipple.

She was so soft. Her flesh giving way to the pressure of my fingers, my thighs, my mouth.

My hair stood on end. Every single one of her touches seared my skin. Her fingertips trailing my stomach. Her tongue scraping mine. The press of her palm on my erection.

Her pulse throbbed fast against my lips. I skimmed my hands down her sides, pulling her stomach to mine, a constant urging to be closer—to find space and fill it. She arched her back. A gasp trapped between our mouths. My fingers dug into the flesh of her ass.

She groaned. "I'm on birth control, and I was cleared at my last screening."

"Me too."

"We don't need a condom if you're okay with that."

I slid my fingers between her wet lips, and she sucked in a shuddering breath as I circled her clit. "I'm okay with that."

She clung to me with her arms around my neck, her face turned down to where my fingers rubbed. I held her with my other arm around her waist savoring the jerks and twitches of her body. Her pleasure mounted, her hold on me tightened, and I kept my rhythm.

"Rem," she breathed.

My name from her mouth, whispered like that—a plea, a promise, a prayer—made me ravenous. I'd never be sated. I'd always be hungry for her.

A hunger to devour. To *be* devoured.

I plunged my fingers inside of her, needing to feel her spasm. When she did, I held her until she stopped shivering, until she pulled my mouth to hers and kissed me slow and lingering. She let her head fall back against the wall. The manifestation of my fantasies with her breasts rising and falling with each breath between her parted lips.

I slipped my hand from between her legs and put my glistening fingers in my mouth and sucked her taste from them.

Her half-lidded eyes widened slightly before she said, "And you said your slutty days were behind you."

"Yeah, okay," I admitted, "I do like that."

Taking hold of my hand, she led me into my bedroom. I sat on the edge of my bed, loving all the signs of her in this place—her smell on my bedding, her phone charger on my bedside table, her lotion on top of my dresser. I loved the way she placed a hand on my shoulder as she put a knee on either side of my hip, straddling me. I loved the feel of her hips under my hands, and way she lifted her chin back for me to kiss her neck.

"I love you," I whispered into the heat of her skin.

She cupped my cheek, looking down at me. "I love you too."

So many of my jagged edges fit back into place. Pieces that were never meant to reconnect. Wounds that hadn't healed right, somehow had found their cure.

Holding my gaze, she placed the head of my cock at her entrance then lowered, taking me inside of her, slowly. Tortuously. Ecstasy.

With nothing between us, just the slip of her skin on mine, we moved together. She set the pace and I savored it. The languid sway of our bodies, her grip in my hair, the taste of salt on her skin. There wasn't any rush, just this. Despite how hard I was, the demand for release was quieter than my need for her.

For a moment it was too much, everything inside of me. The pressure building in my chest. Marveling at her, at being here together, that, despite everything, we were in love. That we would be together for the rest of our days, because nothing could break us again. Not with all the healing and growing we'd done. If we could get past *everything* there was nothing that we couldn't overcome.

Want was too small of a word for how I felt for her.

But yearning, fuck, I knew yearning.

I knew it in my fibers. It was weaved into my connective tissues—so much a part of me, she had to be able to see it.

She pressed her forehead to mine, our movements growing more urgent.

"I love you," she gasped between kisses.

I could only growl my response, incapable of forming words when I could only feel. She gave into the force of my hands moving us closer, harder, my hips thrusting up to meet hers. The noises she made with each movement had me inches away from release. I could barely hold back, wanting her to come with me. To fall over the edge, clinging to one another as we fell.

When I didn't think I could take anymore, she cried out, her pussy twitching and convulsing around my shaft.

I groaned into her chest. My arms wrapped around her back. I spilled inside of her, completely and totally satisfied.

Chapter Thirty-Five

Alicia

"A week?!" Sadie yelled into the phone. The speaker broke out under the strain of her high-pitched demand.

I cringed. It was early morning, I'd left with Furgie first thing to go for a walk, while I waited for Town Hall to open so I could submit the petition. The weekend's events were still carrying me on a high, all the way from getting the signatures I needed, to spending Sunday with Remi curled up in front of the fire. To waking up Monday morning knowing that somehow he and I would make everything work.

But there was the less-satisfying task of telling the people in our lives just that and dealing with the fallout of their feelings on it.

Sadie started and stopped a few sentences before she was finally able to say, "You've been fucking your ex for a week."

"Yeah . . . I know. It sounds really bad . . ." I swallowed, trying to strengthen my tone. "And it's not just fucking."

"What"—she made an irritated *hmm* sound then said—"What does that mean?"

"That I . . . love him." Finally saying the words out loud felt good, but also insane.

It took a few beats of silence before Sadie forced out, "Are you okay?"

I blinked down at Furgie as she sniffed a fire hydrant. "Am I okay?"

"Like emotionally, physically, mentally. Like, girl, this is one of the most off-base things I could imagine you doing."

My face distorted into a whole new cringe. If telling Sadie—someone who did not know me and Remi at the time of our divorce—was going this poorly, then I really didn't know how we were going to tell our families. "I'm good."

"Are you?"

"Yes."

Absolutely.

"Well . . . hell, 'Licia." She sighed, and I pictured her hand pressed to her forehead the way she did when she was overwhelmed.

I had one earbud in so that I could chat with her while walking Furgie—which said more about being a woman than the dangers of Grand Ridge. The snow had mostly thawed, and the sandy soil was soft and wet.

"So, what is going on with you and *Remi*?" Sadie drew out all the sounds of his name.

"You don't have to say his name like a dirty word."

"I disagree."

Looking both ways, I crossed the street. The sidewalk led up a sharp hill to the elementary school, and I was a bit winded as I asked, "Are you mad?"

She groaned. "No. Yes. I'm worried . . ." She trailed off and I waited for her to put her thoughts into words. "We didn't know each other when you went through your divorce, but like, I *know*, you know?"

I grunted my understanding.

"Like, he's not just some guy. He's the one that . . . He left his mark. No other guy has ever had a chance with you because of him. And I don't know this man for any other reason than he *hurt* you. And if he does it again . . . I don't want to cause him physical damage. But I will."

I coughed a laugh, my heart melting. "Physical damage?"

"Yes. And don't say *aww*, I'm not being adorable."

"Oh, Sadie, we should do a coaching on how to be threatening."

"Don't. I'm being serious." She might have sounded cute, but her concern for me was real—and I just loved her.

"I'm sorry, Sadie. I hear you."

"Do you? What if *I* told you this?"

My shoulders climbed toward my ears, and I wished I could shrink to the size I actually felt. "I would not be cool about it."

"No, you wouldn't. And you'd be dead to nuts right not to be. You'd be having a come to Jesus talk with me so fast. I'm worried for you."

"I know."

She sniffled. "This is what you want?"

"So badly," I admitted through the tightness in my chest and the vulnerability of admitting it.

"Okay, then what does this mean? Is he moving here?"

"I think I might stay . . ."

"In *Michigan*? Hours away from me?"

"Maybe?"

"I'm going to kill him. He doesn't get to take you away from me."

"It's not just him. I'm really starting to love it here. He offered to move, but I travel for work, so it doesn't make sense for him to uproot his life."

"But it makes sense for you to?" she demanded. "Listen to yourself."

"We haven't fully decided," I argued.

"Okay." She heaved a sigh. "Okay. I don't like this, I think you're being . . . I don't know. Spontaneous and chaotic and reckless."

"Jesus, don't hold back."

"I will not."

I chewed on my lower lip, this was about how I expected this conversation to go but it didn't make it any less uncomfortable.

"But that's who you are, and I love you for being so wildly messy. And I'll have your back . . . always. I'll wear a bridesmaids dress if you marry him *again,* or I'll hold your hand if he makes you cry."

"Sadie," I whispered her name, my throat too tight to say more.

"If he fucks this up, I will wound him."

I let out a watery laugh. I was fighting back my tears like my life depended on it, because she was not going to make me cry standing outside the fence of a playground. When I could trust my voice not to wobble, I said, "That was slightly more threatening."

"Threatening implies that I don't actually mean it."

"How'd I get so lucky?"

"Because amazing people find amazing people."

"Ugh. I freaking love you."

"I freaking love you too."

I started walking back toward my car parked at the library with its giant stone bricks and pillars flanking the front door. It was an incredible building. I didn't know how it ended up being built here but it was obviously loved by the community.

"Congratulations, by the way," she said, her voice a little more normal. My eyebrows shot up.

"Not for whatever the hell is going on with you and *Remi*—"

I rolled my eyes, but only a little.

"I'm not ready for that," she went on. "But for the signatures. I know you wanted this so badly."

"Thank you." I checked my watch. "Speaking of, it's time for me to go submit the petitions. On to the next stage."

"Grab a coffee after to celebrate!"

We said our goodbyes, and Furgie and I piled into my car. I drove the short distance to Town Hall. Promising to be right back, I patted her head before strolling into the building.

When I caught sight of Deb's frowning face, apprehension twisted in my gut.

Shaking her head, she said, "Young lady, we've got a problem."

Chapter
Thirty-Six

Remi

My phone had been buzzing in my scrubs' pocket for a while, but I had my hands full with a particularly grumpy Himalayan named Pickle. The cat's long silky fur was everywhere, big tuffs of it on my clothes and on the exam table. He slipped under my hands as I tried to complete the wellness check. His eyes narrowed accusingly as he hissed warnings my way. The owner, Mrs. Higgins, halfheartedly tried to keep her cat still. Instead, she startled away every time Pickle growled—which was pretty much constantly. Between the buzzing in my pocket, the angry cat and the jingling of the long dangling earrings Mrs. Higgins wore, I was feeling a bit overstimulated.

Finally, I was able to put Pickle back into his carrier while trying to explain my assessment of his health—he was a bit overweight and could use regular grooming visits. I kept having to start and restart my sentences as most of my attention went into not getting bitten.

My grip automatically tightened at a tap on the door, but Nora must have known that the cat would bolt and spoke through the door instead of opening it. "Rem, Alicia is on the phone. Will you be able to speak to her in a few minutes?"

Jerking my head, I forced my voice to not betray the rush of concern that had rushed to the base of my throat. "Yes, we're almost done. Is everything okay?"

"She said she's not in danger, but that it is an urgent matter."

"Is she on hold or should I call her back?"

"She's holding."

A few minutes later, I directed Mrs. Higgins, carrying a growling carrier, to the lobby where Nora took over. In quick, long strides, I closed the distance between me and the blinking phone line where Alicia waited.

I pressed the phone to my ear. "Leese?"

"Rem, I'm so sorry to do this, but I'm desperate."

"What's up?"

"The road commissioner approved a delivery of an excavator to the marsh."

"What the fu—" I cut myself off just in time remembering that there was a client in hearing distance. "How? The sale hasn't even gone through."

"I know. Apparently, the senator was able to push through special permits to allow excavation. Jamison is looking into the legality of all of this, but without a judge stopping everything, I'm kinda fucked."

Something cold and heavy lay on my sternum. The plastic of the handset creaked under the pressure of my grip. "So, that's it? They win?"

Nora and Mrs. Higgins weren't even pretending not to eavesdrop. They hardly broke their eye contact with my profile to blink. Hazel chatting with her client grew nearer, and I must have looked as concerned as I felt because she came to a halt in the office doorway.

"No," Alicia said with certainty. "They're trying to force us to back down. And it's not gonna happen. I handed in the petition this morning. They're scrambling—but so are we. Frost laws haven't been lifted. They don't even own the land yet. I think they're hoping to excavate enough that we don't have anything to fight for, but we are not done. It's bleak, though."

The combination of realism and persistence was enough to make my love for her fill my chest.

Through the receiver, I heard the click of her turn signal as she explained, "Jamison is on his way with contracts, but it's a two-hour drive from Lansing to here. He's trying to get a local judge to place a cease and desist or something, but he doesn't have connections here. I just need time."

"Okay, what do I do?"

"I'm heading there now."

"Is that safe?"

Hazel touched Nora's shoulder whispering, "What's going on?"

"Something to do with the wetlands," Nora answered with an air of someone not wanting to be distracted.

"I'll be live streaming, and I doubt they'll hurt me. I'll probably just be arrested," Alicia answered me.

I snorted a humorless laugh. "Just."

"It'll be fine," she was speaking fast. "I just need you to be prepared to bail me out if Jamison isn't here yet."

I snapped my gaze to meet Nora's and then Hazel's. "You just need to buy some time?"

"That's it," Alicia answered.

"And it's just you against an excavator."

She groaned. "When you say it like that, it sounds incredibly futile. Rem, I will not stop. If I lose"—her voice shook on the word "lose"—"I will know that I did everything in my power to stop this. Do not ask me to give up."

"I would never," I promised. "But I'm coming with you."

"You can't come! I need someone to bail me out!" Her voice rose; the stress of the situation had shortened her patience.

"I'll get that fixed too."

"*Rem.*"

"*Leese.*"

"What are you gonna do?"

My mouth hung open for a moment, not sure exactly what to say until the words formed, "Get arrested with you, I guess."

"That's so . . . foolish."

"I have to hang up. I'll be right there. I love you."

"You shouldn't come. But I love you too."

The click of plastic on plastic broke the otherwise total silence of the room. On the other side of the desk, a couple of clients waited with their pets. Everyone stared directly at me. Waiting.

Rubbing my hand on the back of my neck, I told Hazel, "I have to go."

"What's going on?" Nora asked.

"They're coming to dig up the wetlands."

Someone gasped, but I didn't look to see who.

"They haven't bought it—" Hazel started, but I interrupted her.

"It's sketchy as hell. Alicia's going to try and stop them—I'm gonna go be with her."

"Just the two of you?"

"That's not gonna work." Nora typed furiously on her phone.

I shrugged.

Hazel nodded a couple of times, then pointed down the hall. "Grab some blankets and . . . there's some high vis gear in there. Grab whatever you need."

"Thanks." I pointed to both of Nora and Hazel. "You two be ready to bail us out if we get arrested. I'll pay you back."

Nora only grunted in agreement.

"Okay." Hazel pulled me into a hug. "Be careful."

I turned and started jogging down the hallway, Mrs. Higgins' voice carried behind me. "Ginny, they're goin' after them wetlands . . . I know! No, I just heard about it here at the vet . . ."

I was almost to the marsh when I passed Creger stables and came to a skidding halt before throwing my car into reverse. Stopping just outside of the arena, I texted Brooks.

It didn't take very long to find Everett in his office on the second story of the big barn.

He looked up, his eyebrows raised, as I knocked. "Remi?"

"Hey, I'm sorry to interrupt."

Chapter Thirty-Seven

Alicia

The truck driver delivering the excavator was not impressed by my presence. On my live stream he flailed his hands and called me very unflattering names, but I wouldn't move. One of the benefits of the road frontage was that it didn't have a lot of driveway options. If he dropped the giant piece of machinery just anywhere, it would be at risk of sinking into the mud. Not that that would be a catastrophic issue for the excavator—it could definitely handle some sinking, but the truck driver was still pissed at me.

"Some silly bitch is standin' here," he hollered into his phone. "Nah, she's got her phone out recordin' or some shit."

Considering all the nonsense I'd pulled in the past, I didn't think there was anything more fruitless than what I was currently doing.

The sun was a hazy blotch in the overcast sky. I shivered in my big puffy coat and wished I'd had the foresight to put my snow pants in my car. My toes and fingers were already cold, not dangerously so, but uncomfortable. And there was no way to know how long I'd be out there. At least, he hadn't threatened to call the police. Yet.

"Yeah." He scratched at the high visibility stocking cap he wore over his messy hair. "I can drop it in the road. Where's your operator? It can't just sit in there."

He was still grumbling as he rounded the other side of his trailer, but I couldn't understand him. A bind holding the excavator in place slackened. And a little bit of the foolish hope I'd been holding on to plummeted. One by one the bindings flicked loose, with each one I wondered what I was doing here.

Time. I needed to buy time.

But what was the point? Was there any worse feeling than the feeling of defeat? I sank under it. Overwhelmed by it.

To my left came a consistent thud like stone hitting sand. My eyebrows pinched together. It was familiar, but I couldn't make sense of it, until I turned in the sound's direction.

Wet sand kicked up from the hooves of a gray horse, atop it Remi sat straight backed. His brown corduroy coat unzipped, the bottom caught in the wind. Underneath, his navy blue hoodie strained against the flex of his pecs. The waves of his hair flew back from his face all windswept like a romance novel cover model. He swayed with the movements of the horse's stride in a way that could only be described as suggestive. And his damn thick-ass thighs were beautifully at eye level.

It was all so surreal, and—God help me—hot I was a little concerned that I was experiencing a hypothermia induced hallucination.

He pulled the reigns and slowed, as he neared.

I stood completely still, staring up and up and *up* at him, my eyebrows pulled high on my forehead. In my shocked stupor I'd somehow trained my camera on him and his *steed*.

"Hey, Leese." He grinned down at me rubbing the horses neck, both of their breathing a little labored, steam circling them.

"What are you doing?" I whispered.

"Being a pain in the ass," he whispered back, as if that explained anything.

Louder he called to the truck driver, "Excuse me, sir. I'm going to need you to not unload that. I have the high school equestrian team on their way, and one of the horses might spook. It could be dangerous."

"What?" I laughed.

After letting out a string of expletives, the driver yelled back, "Look, Seabiscuit, I'm unloading this goddamn thing and heading home. Tell your high schoolers to go ride their ponies somewhere else."

"Seabiscuit?" Remi smiled huge and unbothered. "Sir, I'm really sorry, this is where we're practicing our canter. Important stuff cantering. Gotta practice."

The trucker mumbled something under his breath.

"I'm sorry, I didn't hear that."

"I'm unloading this thing."

"But the kids and their *cantering*." I couldn't keep the chuckle out of my voice. This whole thing was ridiculous, and if I wasn't already head over heels for Remi this would have made it happen.

The crunch of dirt under tires joined our little group. Remi's horse shook his head and took a couple of steps to the side at the arrival of a black truck that parked directly behind the semi-trailer.

Throwing his hands up, the trucker exclaimed, "You have got to be shitting me."

Mrs. Creger stuck her head out of the driver's side window. "Buddy, I'm gonna need you to pull forward. You're parked right in the way."

"In the way of what?" His face was bright red, and a vein protruded from his neck.

"Euchre." She flicked her hand as if it was obvious.

"*Euchre?!*"

"Yup, I got a permit, right here. We're going to be lining up for the next quarter mile and playin' a tournament."

Remi pressed a palm to his chest, his head falling back as he laughed at the overcast sky. My mouth hung open, and goosebumps prickled up my arms.

More cars turned on to the dirt road, and the driver cussed a string of swear words I'd never heard in quite that order. He looked like he was going to argue with Mrs. Creger who was yelling at him to watch his language, when more hoof beats on dirt announced the arrival of Brooks' and four teenagers all on horseback trailing behind him. The kids' riding in to save the day was less majestic than Remi's with their thin limbs and uncoordinated movements. But they were absolutely perfect.

Equestrian team and euchre club to save the day.

Beautiful.

Too overwhelmed—my laughter sounding more like sobs—I hid my face in my hand not holding my still-streaming phone.

The driver shook his head in shock, his jaw clenched.

Remi lifted one large shoulder. "Canter practice."

Throwing his arms in the air, the driver finally seemed to give up. "You're all crazy!"

"That may be, but you are still in the way," Deb yelled back.

"I'm movin', lady, I'm movin'."

"Thank you," she said, but her tone did not sound grateful.

A battered, white work truck rumbled toward us from down the road. It slowed to a crawl, and one of the women in Deb's truck bed called out, "Brian, I know you're not here to operate that excavator."

The man who wouldn't sign my petition at Nora's party brought his vehicle to a stop and rolled down the passenger side window. "Gran, it's my job."

"Well, you'll have to find something else to do today, he's packing it back up."

"This is ridiculous," he grumbled, casting a glare toward me and Remi. "I'm just trying to do my job."

"Me too," I shot back to which Brian rolled his eyes.

He turned back to his grandma. "You should go home. All you ladies, you're gonna get sick in this cold."

"We'll be just fine," his grandma answered.

"Does Grandpa know you're out here?"

"You know what, why don't you go on over to our place and tell him for me? See what he has to say about all of this."

Heaving an irritated sigh, he rolled his window back up and drove away.

"Hey, Remi." One of the high schoolers brought her horse to a stop next to his gray horse.

"Hey, Crystal, thanks for being here."

"Conner and a couple of other kids couldn't get permission from their parents, so it's just us."

He had that smile that melted my insides—all crinkly eyes, and white teeth. "That's fine, you were enough. He's tying it back down and driving away."

"Really?"

"Yeah."

Remi's midnight gaze met mine—an ever-expanding universe of emotions and promises in their depths. Happy tears trickled down my cheeks, wondering how life could deliver so many beautiful and unexpected outcomes.

"You did it, Leese. You bought time." He swung a leg over the saddle and lowered to the ground.

I flung an indistinct hand at the general chaos of white-haired ladies in giant coats and hats heaving and propping each other into the back of pickup trucks and sharing blankets as they dealt cards onto TV trays.

Then I pointed to four teenagers looking like they didn't know what to do with their hands or where to look, and like the most incredible future.

"I didn't do this," I sobbed, my voice raspy. I pressed a frozen hand to his cheek. At some point I must have dropped my phone because I wasn't holding it anymore. "That was them. That was you."

"You gave us something to rally for."

"I can't stop crying. I must look ridiculous."

He pulled me against him, my puffy coat bunching. His lips were hot on my cold forehead. "You look perfect."

Sobbing and laughing, I hid my face in the rough fabric of his coat. "How is this happening?"

Instead of answering, he held me tighter and pressed a kiss to my temple. It was good. It was more than good. It was solid. And I trusted it implicitly.

I trusted him.

I trusted me.

Pulling his mouth to mine, I savored the feel—claiming his kiss as if it were a trophy for my victory. As if everything was as simple as his touch, and as satisfying as the taste of his lips. As if, just like the challenges between us, everything would work out.

Chapter
Thirty-Eight

Remi

In the forty minutes after the semi hauled the excavator away, Brooks actually did run canter practice—because he was nothing if not efficient—and Alicia and I joined in a game of euchre before we were eliminated embarrassingly fast. Neither of us could stop laughing about it. Shortly after, it was decided to be "too gosh darn cold" to remain on the side of the road.

Brooks offered to stay behind for another hour or so to be sure the driver didn't come back.

"Thank you so much," Alicia shivered out.

And even though her car was parked on the shoulder, she sat in front of me in the saddle to return Stone to the stables. The soft curve of her seated against my groin was hard to ignore, despite the trail of high school students following us. She leaned back against my chest, putting her clove-scented hair under my nose. One of my hands held the reins loosely, and the other was wrapped protectively around her waist despite the easy pace we kept.

Turning her head, she asked, "How did you do all of this?"

"I was only responsible for the kids and horses. I'm guessing Mrs. Higgins got the euchre club activated," I said, trying and failing to ignore how close her mouth was to mine. It would be easy to lean a few inches down and kiss her, but again, the children.

"I want to be just like those ladies when I grow up."

I hugged her even tighter against my chest. "I don't see you calming with age."

She snorted. "Absolutely not."

"We don't even have to make bail."

"That really is a relief. I hate getting arrested."

My eyebrows shot up. "You have been?"

"Not for work. It was recreational."

I nudged her with my thigh. "Continue . . ."

"Not in front of the children."

At the stables, she helped get the horse brushed down and ready for the night. I couldn't take my eyes off her, the easy way she made conversation with the kids and retold Emmett and his business partner, Missy, the story of the showdown—earning a couple of hearty laughs from him. Missy's pale eyes flicked to mine and Alicia's entwined hands, and the two women shared a nonverbal conversation that ended with Missy's eyebrow raised very high, and Alicia blushing.

I squeezed her hand and lowered to whisper in her ear, "Are you okay? Should I limit the PDA?"

She pulled back to glare up at me. "Absolutely not," she answered at normal volume.

My stomach flipped, and a smile spread across my face. "Okay."

Emmett and Missy promised to join us in celebrating at the Pour House after finishing a few things, as Alicia and I waved goodbye before sliding into my SUV.

When we arrived downtown, we had to park a few blocks away and it seemed that most of the town was inside the little restaurant. It was a staple of the older generations in Grand Ridge, so it was the obvious choice of the euchre club. As we neared the front door, the sounds of people gathered inside grew louder and tumbled out when we swung the door open. We had hardly stepped inside, when a cry rang out. People clapped and called out from every corner of the building. I fell behind Alicia, joining in with the applause.

She waved a hand over head, her smile so bright she practically glowed. She reached a gloved hand behind her back, and I didn't know if she was offering it to me because she wanted my support or just my touch, but I placed my palm in hers following her further into the restaurant. People pulled us into group hugs and patted her on the back.

Nora slid out from a booth followed by Hazel. Both Alicia and I took the opportunity to take off our coats and gloves tossing them into the green vinyl booth.

Alicia cried out, "Oh my God! Did you hear about what happened?!" as they neared.

"It's all anyone can talk about," Nora said.

"The livestream was hilarious," Hazel added handing Alicia a cider and me a beer.

Flicking her eyes to our joined hands, Nora smirked. "And that kiss was hot as hell."

The blood drained from Alicia's face.

A shiver ran down my spine, and my stomach twisted sickeningly. I cleared my throat. "Our kiss was on it?"

Nora went to answer, but Alicia turned to me, her face stricken. "My mom follows that page."

Hazel and Nora only looked confused for a moment, when Hazel's eyes widened with understanding. "Your moms don't know?!"

I set our drinks back on the table, snatching our coats in the same motion. "We gotta go make some phone calls."

We'd gotten ourselves pretty psyched up on the drive home, but actually waiting for my mom to answer my call kinda sucked. Alicia had her phone pressed to her ear too and stood when the call connected.

"Hey, Mom," Alicia spoke into her phone, walking toward my kitchen while I held my phone to my ear listening to it ring for my own mom to answer the other end. I rubbed at the back of my neck, where my anxiousness was tightening my muscles.

Alicia's voice was confident and unwavering, but I was sure just like me her mom knew it for the tell it was—Alicia was at least a little nervous too. "You know how you've always said that you will always love me . . . Well . . . what I'm about to tell you will test the boundaries of that statement . . ."

I snorted, but my smile turned into a cringe when my mom answered.

"Rem, I was just thinking about you!"

"You were?" I asked, relieved to ease into the conversation a bit.

"I. Was."

Just like when I'd thought I'd gotten away with sneaking out of the house when I was sixteen, alarm bells sounded inside my head.

"Tell me why," she went on, "I just saw a video come across the page of that cute little bar in your town, of you climbing down from a horse and kissing your ex-wife."

"You saw that?"

"I did."

Sighing, I sent a silent curse to the Internet.

"It's a wild story. You're not even gonna believe it."

"Considering I don't believe what I saw with my own eyes, you might as well tell me a story."

"Remember when I told you someone was moving into the other side of my duplex?"

"Yeah."

"Guess who it was."

She chuckled a little as she said, "You have got to be shitting me."

When we'd exhausted every angle of shock, and outright disbelief we ended the conversation, and I stood to join Alicia in the kitchen. She sat on the countertop, typing something out on her phone.

I ran a hand up her thigh, planting myself between her knees. "Texting Sadie?"

"Yeah," Alicia said putting her phone on the counter next to her.

"Telling her about everything with your mom?"

Alicia rested her hands on my shoulders. "Yeah. She did that mom thing where she isn't mad, just disappointed."

I pulled her to the edge of the counter wrapping my arms around her waist—appreciating the way she arched her back and pressed her tits into my chest. "I'm sorry, Leese."

"How'd it go with your mom?"

"She thinks it's all too kismet for it not to be divine intervention."

Grinning, Alicia brushed her lips across mine. "Will you have her tell the divine thank you for me?"

Deepening our kiss, we fell into the rhythm of our quickening heartbeats. The heady demand of our bodies. Giving ourselves to something as simple and complex as surrendering to love.

Epilogue

Alicia

Election Day

B enji's Place erupted, drowning out the last few words Ben spoke into the microphone. I flung my arms around Remi, but he hoisted me up, and I got to see the celebration from above. A sea of my new friends and neighbors all cheering, jumping, and hugging one another because the canvassing and phone calls had worked. It had been a rough few months, but it. Had. Worked.

The marsh was safe.

Tears stung my eyes as I returned Sadie's huge smile, her mouth moving in what looked like the phrase, *Baddest bitch*, but I couldn't hear her over the roar. Next to her, Jamison—former? fuckboy lawyer—clapped and grinned down at her. I was still getting used to the new history there, and the way it all came about was almost as crazy as how things had gone with me and Remi.

I was so happy she was here to see why I had fallen in love with this place. And to see me and Remi together. In love.

Wild.

He set my feet back on the ground placing a kiss on my forehead, and my cheekbone, then my lips.

Contentedness was such an underrated feeling. It filled every inch of my body, warming me. It felt like I must be glowing, I was so happy.

He spoke quietly in my ear, "Congratulations. I'll never stop being impressed by you. Truly unstoppable."

My throat was almost too tight to speak through. "Don't make me cry. Not in front of all of these people."

"All right," he said in the tone of someone who thought I was being silly.

Slowly, the chant of "Speech!" rang out over all the other noises.

I blinked, and pressed my ring fingers under my eyes, willing them to dry before I moved away from the shelter of Remi's chest. With one last deep breath full of his clean scent, I straightened my spine and turned toward the little stage. Ben extended his hand down as I climbed the one stair, which I took even though I probably wouldn't trip, but it was better safe than sorry.

The microphone ended up in my hands, and I turned to face the crowd. I had never struggled to speak in public before, but in that moment my mind went blank. I couldn't seem to string together any words. In the course of my career, I'd been lucky enough to give some version of this speech multiple times. I wanted it to be different this time, because everything *was* different. This little town with its rumor mills, and cutthroat euchre players, its quirks and heart, was the place I had planted my roots.

Against all odds, Grand Ridge had created the perfect scenario for me to find Remi again. For him and me to give into all the love between us.

If there was a way to tell these people how they had influenced me, how proud I was to be their new addition because they had given so much of themselves to this cause. I hoped I would find the way to say any of that.

I sighed, and like always my eyes found Remi. His hands tucked deep in the pockets of his jeans, his feet shoulder width apart perfectly balanced—as if he were ready to carry some of the pressure I was putting on myself.

"I hope you all realize," I began, "what we've done here. Future generations will know this land the way it is now, because of us. Our fight over the past few months did not have a guaranteed outcome. Because of you, we spread our message and the voters showed up to say, *This nature is worth preserving*."

Nora let out a *woo*, and I smiled when I found her standing next to her sister, Olivia. She had returned without her fiancé, and the rumors were circulating about the status of that relationship. Brooks was near too, his gaze locked onto her—the longing in his eyes was something I understood. The way it consumed a person to want someone. Need another person. It was scary and intense.

It twisted my already heightened emotions to see him so unguarded in his longing.

I didn't know him or Olivia well, but I hoped for them. Because I had become someone who did that.

Hope for love.

"There's really nothing to say but thank you for your time and effort. Your passion."

Remi's eyes were so dark in this lighting, they looked black. Endlessly deep. Containing everything. A tear escaped to roll down my cheek, as I spoke directly to him. "I couldn't be more proud to call this place home."

Cheers broke out again.

I didn't bother making my way to the stairs. Instead, I took two steps to the end of the stage and landed directly into Remi's arms knowing he'd have me.

Knowing that I had him.

The End

Would you like more Remi and Alicia?

Enjoy this free download of my first iteration of their "I love you" and meet cute.

https://dl.bookfunnel.com/841bnkmswp

Thank Yous

This book took me on the longest journey of any book I've ever worked on. There was a lot of help along the way.

First, I'd like to thank my editors: Kimberly with Revision Division, thank you for your insight on the story. It was a huge help in getting me to dig deeper on the details and characters. Heather with Simply Spellbound Edits, your corrections to the grammar of my stories is immensely appreciated. I also REALLY appreciate all of the comments you make along the way. I cherish every "LOL". THANK YOU!

To the boundlessly talented Kate Prior. Reader, when I tell you she designs my covers, I mean it. I have the hardest time picturing the cover of a book, and Kate always comes to me with an answer. I love you, Kate! Also, big I couldn't do this without you talking through all of my story issues—some of the best conversations of my life.

My critique group, Smut Coven, brought so much enthusiasm as I shared this book. Every week, they sat through multiple chapters and gave me invaluable feedback and confidence that what I was trying to do was working. I don't know how anyone writes without a Smut Coven. I feel like the luckiest writer ever.

Then there's the non-writer helpers in my life. My husband listened to me lament endlessly about this detail or that, while giving me a helpful, "Well, it is very engaging" as input. He's funny and smart, and my favorite person to be with. He's always trying his best even when the content is out of his normal wheelhouse. Thank you for your support, Andrew!

To my mom, thank you for letting me read chapters I'm working on out loud to you and laughing at all the right places. Remember your promise: if you read the spicy scenes, lie to me.

My dear Nell, you have cheerlead this book more than you know. There were so many moments that I doubted myself, because that's what I do, and your telling me that I was so silly and this is the best book I've written really means the world to me! You're beautiful, sweet, smart, and nice! Also, thanks for all the veterinarian input.

Patty! You are such a ray of sunshine. I'm so lucky to have your support. Everyone deserves someone like you endlessly in their corner. Thanks for meeting me and deciding that we were meant to be the bestest of friends.

Finally, thanks to my kids. Just keep being wild, creative, monsters. I love being your mom.

Entirely Yours

Chapter 1

Tessa

I held my steering wheel so tightly it felt like it or my fingers would break. Little-by-little, I convinced myself to relax. Outside my driver's side window, cars sped past me on the freeway as I focused on the long grass swaying in the wind they left in their wake. My heart still raced even though at this point, I was technically safe.

"It's just a flat tire," I whispered over the roar of blood in my ears. The pop had been loud, but it hadn't sent my car into an uncontrollable fishtail or anything. "It was just an exciting few seconds, that's all. It's done now."

"Shit," I hissed, realizing it was now my job to change my first ever tire on the shoulder as cars screamed past me.

I decided I had at least sixty more seconds to calm the fuck down.

The freeway noise was so much louder outside of my vehicle, undoing all the deep breathing I'd done to lower my shoulders from my earlobes. Totes and boxes I'd just rented from the Darling Civic Players costume closet were sitting at a steep angle on the embankment. I was about one semi away from it all toppling down the hill. I had five whole pennies to produce *The Music Man*—my least favorite play ever, but we already had the script—for the high school's Spring play, and I needed those costumes to remain pristine in order to get my deposit back.

I'd slipped on my way back up to the road, leaving half of my bright pink leggings and hypno-kitty tank top covered in mud.

But I'd pulled my spare tire out of its hidey-hole, along with the plus-sign-shaped-tool-thingy and diamond-shaped jack. I laid them out on the ground behind my bumper to assess. How exactly they should work? It took a few seconds to decide that I needed YouTube University for this one. I begged to no one, that I had somehow blown my tire in a pocket of cell service—I didn't. The west coast of Michigan's lower peninsula was fresh with cherry orchards and asparagus, but not cell service.

I was so close to Grand Ridge, my home. And where I stood a chance of a friend or cousin driving by and offering help.

"No." I squared my shoulders. "I can do this. None of this is brain surgery."

The jack was surprisingly heavy in my hands. The metal pinched the pads of my fingers just a little as I wondered if there was a top or bottom or if it was universal. I chewed my lower lip and walked to the side of my car irritated as hell that I didn't know how to do this. Twenty-nine years on this earth, eighteen years of education, and all I could think in this moment was, *I need my dad.*

Behind me, a vehicle crunched on the rocks and gravel at the side of the road, stopping me mid-crouch. The sun reflected off of the windshield, making it impossible to see the driver, but I recognized the teal Jeep, unfortunately.

Emiliano Vazquez.

He slid out of the driver's side door, with a serious set to his lips and sunglasses covering his eyes. His thick, curly black hair ended just below his jaw. He wasn't much taller than my five feet six inches. His frame was densely muscular under a tank-top that had the vintage MTV logo on it, tucked into those slutty shorts men wore—the ones that showed at least half of their thighs.

In a few hours the sun would set and the weather would be too cold for either of our outfits. But for now, we could pretend it was almost summer.

And despite being my sworn enemy, he did in fact pull off of the slutty shorts very well.

He taught math at the high school where I taught English. The math of it all was a red flag—to each their own, but math was the worst. Also, the man was incapable of dumping used coffee grounds into the trash—all of those muscles and he couldn't even lift the coffee maker lid. And even though we *technically* didn't have assigned parking spots, every other month he'd park in mine. It happened too often to be unintentional, which he didn't deny when I called him on it, but he also didn't confess.

Monster.

He took easy steps toward me. "Hey, I saw your tire blow. Are you okay?"

"You saw it?"

"Yeah, I was driving behind you." He pointed down the freeway and then over his shoulder, explaining, "Going from exit-to-exit, and then entrance to get turned around, took a few minutes. I wanted to...make sure you're good."

"Did you know it was me?"

He pushed his sunglasses into his hair and narrowed his dark brown eyes at me. "I don't think I could mistake your car for anyone else's."

I raised my eyebrows in acceptance. My car wasn't exceptional, but it had a sticker on it of Bella on Edward's back that read, *My other ride is Edward Cullen.*

"I guess you're good, then?" he asked again.

Jerking my head in something like confirmation, I gripped the jack in front of me with both hands. It was getting really heavy.

"So"—he pointed over his shoulder at his Jeep—"I should just go."

"Mmm," I hummed with my lips pinched tight, knowing that if I let them open, I'd say something like, *No, don't go. Save me.*

It was these moments that I wished I could be less principled. It didn't happen often, just sometimes.

It was asinine.

Was he really to blame for the high school's budget decisions for clubs and sports?

No, but he could *try*. When they threw money at him, he could be like, *We can use the same bullhorn I yelled at the kids with last year. Give ten more dollars to the theater instead.*

But he didn't do that. And I didn't need to be cool with him.

"Okay, if you've got it all taken care of." His hand fell to his thigh with a slap.

So, slutty.

It distracted me enough that my guard dropped to call after his back. "Do you actually know how to do it?"

"Change a tire?" He planted his feet to face me with his arms crossed over his chest.

Great arms. Visibly—he was very pleasing.

"Don't say it like it's embarrassing to not know," I argued.

He sighed the beleaguered sigh of someone who didn't expect a fight.

It was like he didn't even know me.

"I want to know what you mean by *it*," he explained. "I know how to do lots of *it's*. I *do it*, all the time."

I pursed my lips, fighting back a laugh. Realization dawning on his face.

He shook his head. "You're as bad as the students."

"It was just a little braggy. I don't need to know that much about your personal life. Should I report this?"

"I think administration is sick of hearing you complain."

"I have grievances!"

"As we all know."

"God forbid a woman speak her mind"—

"Close the floodgates. We don't need to do this," he interrupted, but I kept going.

—"I'm not going to keep quiet because it would make it easier on you"—

"No one would accuse you of making things easy."

—"Just because everyone else worships you and that concussion-ridden sport"—

"Jesus, at this rate, we could fill the tire with your hot air."

—"Doesn't mean I'm going to"—

"Damn it, Tessa, do you want help or not?"

"No."

"Okay"—

"But I need it." It pained me to admit, "I don't know how to do this."

His dark eyes softened around the edges, and I wondered if I'd ever seen eyelashes as long as his.

He took a step closer, taking hold of the jack clutched in my fingers and lifted it with much more ease than I had been capable of. I turned my face up to meet his gaze. I'd never been this near to him—he smelled so. Fucking. Good. Something slightly citrus and woodsy.

It might have been my imagination, but it seemed like his voice lowered with a new scrape of grit. It rolled through me like a thunderstorm as he offered, "I can do it for you. Or I can teach you."

Marty Vee in the Wild

M arty Vee is the midwestern gal who is going to banter her steamy contemporary small town into only one bed, time after time. The friends will become lovers, and so will the enemies.

She lives in the Mitten State with her introverted husband, two feral children, the fluffiest house cat, and her tender-hearted rescue dog.

She loves singing (constantly) and meandering hikes through the woods.

Check Out More of My Books At
https://martyvee.com/books-2/

Vee is for Romance Readers Group
https://www.facebook.com/groups/1161878791021065

The Tiktok
https://www.tiktok.com/@martyveeauthur

Instagram
https://www.instagram.com/martyveeauthor/

Romance Writer's Therapy Podcast

https://romancewriterstherapy.buzzsprout.com/